An Instance of Justice

An Instance of Justice

Gene A. Zach

NPI

Northwest Publishing, Inc.
Salt Lake City, Utah

NPI

An Instance of Justice

All rights reserved.
Copyright © 1995 Northwest Publishing, Inc.

Reproduction in any manner, in whole or in part,
in English or in other languages, or otherwise
without written permission of the publisher is prohibited.

This is a work of fiction.
All characters and events portrayed in this book are fictional,
and any resemblance to real people or incidents is purely coincidental.
For information address: Northwest Publishing, Inc.
6906 South 300 West, Salt Lake City, Utah 84047

JAC 6.28.94

Edited by: Ann Cude

PRINTING HISTORY
First Printing 1995

ISBN: 1-56901-379-9

NPI books are published by Northwest Publishing, Incorporated,
6906 South 300 West, Salt Lake City, Utah 84047.
The name "NPI" and the "NPI" logo are trademarks belonging to
Northwest Publishing, Incorporated.

PRINTED IN THE UNITED STATES OF AMERICA.
10 9 8 7 6 5 4 3 2 1

One

Somewhere in the distance a rooster welcomed the dawning of a new day. It was the early morning of a midsummer day in 1945. The moonlight, which had bathed the darkness of the night, was receding. The sun's rays curled over the horizon, awakening nature.

Sunbeams came to rest on the tousled hair of a young boy asleep in an old farmhouse located in the rural area of a small midwestern town. The sunbeams dissipated, producing a spectacular glow, awakening the boy from a deep, dream-filled sleep.

The boy stirred as visions of cowboys on bucking horses and bulls chasing clowns focused in his mind. His extremities jerked, he inhaled deeply and was suddenly fully alert. Instantly Roy Lee remembered that today was the day he had been waiting for. The floor creaked as he jumped out of bed and hopped on one leg, pulling on his bib overalls. Excitement filled his sleepy eyes. On his ninth birthday earlier in the year, his father had promised to take him to the county rodeo to celebrate his birthday. Today was the opening performance. He had anxiously awaited this day for almost six months. Even though most of his friends on the surrounding farms had been to the rodeo, he never had. He had listened intently to their recounts of the excitement in the grandstand and the action in the arena and had longed to share their experiences.

In the next room Al was awakened by the sounds emanating from Roy Lee's room. At first he became irritated. Why is that kid up so early, it isn't even daylight yet, he thought. Then a ray of anticipation welled up inside him. Today he was going to take his son to the county rodeo at Carville. Even though he hadn't been there since he was a child, his pulse quickened as he remembered the excitement he had shared with his father. He had been thrilled by the bullriding and bulldogging events, but what had fascinated him the most had been the calf-roping competition. When he had gotten home he took a rope from the tool shed and fashioned a crude noose in one end. Mimicking the cowboy's slow deliberate pace, he walked up to the barnyard gate and peered through the rails at the young heifers contentedly chewing their cud. A smile crossed Al's face as he remembered the look of disbelief in the eyes of those young cows when he first threw the rope at them. They scattered and were so elusive that even though he repeatedly tried, he never did rope one of them.

Al reached across the sleeping body of his wife, Mary, and turned the alarm clock so he could read the dial. "Ah," he sighed as he saw that it would be fifteen minutes before the alarm went off. He let his arm fall softly on her shoulder and his hand came to rest gently on her breast. She was lying in a fetal position with her back toward him. He brought his body close to hers, making full contact. She was soft and warm and as he pressed closer, a contented murmur escaped her lips.

Al had first met Mary when he was twenty-six years old.

He had been a farmhand and had not had the time, let alone the money, to court many young ladies. He had met her at a country dance when she was sixteen years old. He had fallen in love with her the first time their eyes met. Her hair was long and black with a natural wave. Her eyes seemed to sparkle. They were almond in color with long black eyelashes.

Their romance had been a whirlwind. Every night, after spending long hours in the field, he would sit with her on the back porch of her house. The swing would move in a lazy tempo as he told her of his love. On Saturday nights they would go to one of the surrounding communities to a square dance. They would square dance, waltz, and two-step till the wee hours in the morning. On Sunday, she would pack a picnic lunch and they would spread a blanket amid the shade of a large oak tree and make plans for their future. One Sunday afternoon he noted her pensive mood. She looked so pretty in her bright gingham dress with her hair in a single braid. When he had asked her what was on her mind she had replied in a faltering, desperate voice, "I think I'm pregnant." Two emotions had surged within him—love and fear. How could he possibly support a family? The twenty-five cents an hour he made as a farm laborer barely covered the necessities of life even though he lived with his parents and paid no rent. But his love for her defied all reason. He tenderly took her in his arms and whispered in her ear, "Will you marry me?"

"Yes," she whispered in a half sob and half giggle.

They were married on a cool September afternoon. Al contracted with a local landowner to sharecrop a 160-acre farm. The benevolent owner let them live in an abandoned farmhouse located on the farm, free of rent.

The loud creak startled Al. He looked across the room and saw Roy Lee opening the bedroom door, something he was usually forbidden to do. "Didn't your alarm go off?" he tentatively asked. Al looked at the clock and realized that he had fallen back to sleep. "You go on downstairs, we'll be down in a minute."

Al gently shook his wife. "Time to rise and shine."

"Are any of the kids up?" she asked.

"Only Roy Lee. I haven't heard the other two stirring yet."

As Mary got out of bed and slipped off her nightgown, the sight of her lean supple body stirred a desire within him. She sensed a thrill of excitement as he tenderly put his arms around her nude body and held her tightly. Their lovemaking was gentle, yet compassionate, both aware of each other's needs.

As Al descended the stairs he heard the clanging of milk buckets. Roy Lee was standing by the back door with a milk bucket in each hand. "Why are you so fired up to do your chores so quickly this morning?" Al asked. "You got a bee in your britches?"

"Have you forgot? You promised to take me to the rodeo today and I don't want to be late."

Al smiled as he picked up two farm caps lying on the kitchen table. He shoved one of the caps down over Roy Lee's uncombed hair. It was too big and almost covered his eyes. It caused his ears to stick out. Al laughed and, patting Roy Lee on his rear, said, "Let's get going."

The screen door slammed behind them as they stepped down from the back porch. They walked side by side down the crooked path that led to the old barn. It had once been red but the weathering of time had turned it to silver-gray. One of the hinges on a side door was missing, letting the door hang at an angle as if in pain. A row of pigeons perched on the gable cooed in disharmony. The early morning sun rays reflected a brilliance of colors off the shiny tin roof.

Eddies of dust rose up behind them as they walked down the dry dirt path. The lush green foliage of spring and early summer had disappeared and was being replaced by the colors of autumn. The once-supple stems of foxtail growing by the side of the barn were now dry and crisp, unbending in the breeze. "Got the makin's for a nice day," Al said, "but we could sure use some rain."

As they neared the barn Roy Lee ran ahead, saying, "I'll get the corn and oats, you can throw down the hay." As he found his way through the barn to the grain room in the back, his nostrils were filled with the sweet smell of fresh alfalfa hay that had been put in the loft the week before. It would probably be the last cutting since it was so dry. He filled the two grain buckets, one with corn, the other with oats. It was his job to place a half gallon each of corn and oats in the six feeding boxes located in front of the milking stalls. Meanwhile, Al, with pitchfork in hand, was dropping large bunches of hay into the manger below. Four black mules shoved each other, jockeying for the best position.

As Roy Lee finished distributing the rations of grain to the feeding boxes, he was unaware that Al had silently descended the ladder from the hay mow. "I got yah," Al said, as he grabbed Roy Lee in a bear hug from the back. Roy Lee giggled and wrestled free. He enjoyed the physical contact with his dad. "Better watch out," he said, "I'm nine years old now, I'll be able to take you down before too long." Al reached out and turned the oversized cap on Roy Lee's head sideways so the bill stuck out over one ear. "That'll be the day," he said, smiling.

They could hear the cows lowing behind the barn, impatiently waiting for the barn door to open so they could get to the grain. Al untied the rope holding the sliding door. As it slid open on the track, six hungry cows with taut, milk-filled udders crowded into the milking area. Each cow knew the stall where she belonged. After the cows had begun to eat the grain, Roy Lee asked his father how the cows knew which stall to go in. "Just like us," Al replied, "we always sit in the same place at the kitchen table every meal time."

The six milking short-horn cattle were content and stood quietly while Al and Roy Lee squirted the fresh milk into the clean, silver milk buckets. Al was very proud of Roy Lee; not many nine-year-olds could milk a cow so well. Three barn cats were lined up along the back wall of the barn, hoping for a handout. Al was milking a big old Holstein cow. He turned one of her teats sideways and said, "I bet I can hit the black cat in the face before you can." He squeezed the teat, sending a stream of milk about ten feet, hitting the black cat directly in the face. The cat immediately stuck out its tongue, trying to catch the warm milk in mid-air. "I'll get the yellow one," Roy Lee squealed in delight.

Little did Al realize that the happiness and pleasure he found in his family would soon be shattered. In the years ahead he would look back on this day and remember the chain of events that occurred, changing the lives of his family forever.

Just as she was coming down the stairs, Mary heard the back screen door bang shut. She looked out the window and saw the two of them walking toward the barn together, each with a milk bucket swinging at his side. She was warmed by a flush of pride—her two special men, husband and oldest son. Al had swept her off her feet when they had first met. She had begged her brothers into letting her tag along with them to the Saturday night dance in Laynard. As they entered the Legion Hall where the dance was being held, she saw him standing in the middle of the dance floor with four other young men. His tight-fitting Levis hung low on his hips. The sleeves on his white shirt were rolled up, exposing the golden suntan on his forearms. He had left the two top buttons open, exposing the black curly hair on his chest. He was considered the most handsome bachelor in Laynard. He was short and had well-formed muscles which were the result of the strenuous farm work he did. He combed his black hair straight back, accentuating his angular face. His eyes were always filled with a mischievous gleam. All of her friends were moonstruck over him. They were always asking her how far he tried to go when they were parked late at night on the street in front of her house. She had acted innocent, but to this day could still feel the passion he aroused in her as he whispered in her ear and tenderly caressed her body.

She smiled as she remembered how proud he was of his two front gold teeth. He had been in a fist fight when he was younger and had fractured the teeth, which resulted in two gold caps. They became his trademark. Many of the local residents referred to him as the boy with the gold front teeth.

The arguments they had were usually a result of his drinking. He enjoyed going out with his friends, visiting bars, and flirting with the young ladies. Most of this had stopped after they were married, but occasionally he would buy a fifth of Old Crow and hide it in the corncrib. She could always smell the liquor on his breath when he had taken a "snort" but seldom commented, knowing how defensive he could be at times.

They had been married by a justice of the peace. Her mother had taken in the waist of a hand-me-down dress from an older sister. It fit her very snug, accenting her hips and the slight bulging of her stomach. Al had worn his father's suit. It fit perfectly after his mother had altered the length of the legs. She carried six red roses that Al had picked from the bushes behind his parents' house. A photographer took their picture and it appeared in the Laynard weekly newspaper. Many people commented what a lovely couple they made.

They struggled during the early years of their marriage. Al was lucky to get a job as a tenant farmer, but there never seemed to be enough money even for the necessities. Her parents couldn't help them financially since her father was a dirt farmer and she was the youngest of thirteen children. Al's parents helped them some, at first, with food and clothing, but Al was too stubborn to accept charity. Hard work had enabled them to survive those beginning years. With long hours and a team of mules, Al had profitably cultivated crops of corn and oats for the owner of the farm. He had a natural talent working the soil and seemed to know the exact time of the year to plant or to plow. He tended the livestock with loving care. In the cold of the winter he would bring the new-born farm animals into the house and place them in boxes around the pot-bellied stove, warming them so they would have a better chance at life. He would whisper gently in the ear of a young heifer enduring the pangs of birth of her first calf. He quickly became known in the community as a good farmer and was highly respected.

Al had an innate love for his fellow man. He was always

ready to lend a helping hand to a neighbor in need. One fall day during corn shucking time, the next-door neighbor broke his leg when he fell off the barn he was mending. Al got three other farmers to help and the four of them, leaving the corn in their own fields, harvested the man's crop.

The first year they were married and moved onto the farm, Al had plowed up a large plot of fallow ground adjacent to the barn. In the spring, with Mary at his side, they had planted long rows of garden vegetables. Mary tended the garden and as the plants grew she kept the rows free of weeds and the dirt freshly hoed. She spent many hot summer days canning quart after quart of fresh vegetables which filled their table in the coming months of winter.

Bounding footsteps on the back porch startled Mary from her thoughts. The back kitchen door opened and Roy Lee's face appeared. "Pa said to tell you we have the milking done and as soon as we separate the cream and finish the chores we'll be ready for breakfast."

Mary quickly stood up from the kitchen table. Why do I daydream so much when there's work to be done? she thought. She lifted one of the lids off the wood-burning range and saw only embers remaining from the fire that Al made for her before they had left to do the chores. She added more kindling and blew vigorously, causing ashes to fly back into her face. To her satisfaction, a small flame burst forth and soon there was a crackling blaze. She placed the lid back on the range and pulled a large mixing bowl from the cupboard. She was going to bake sour milk biscuits for her two special men. With a wooden spoon she mixed the ingredients together, then with her hands kneaded the dough until it reached a rubbery consistency. Covering the bowl with a wet cloth, she set it on top of the warming oven on the range.

She opened the icebox door, noting that the ice had almost melted. She made a mental note to tell Al that they needed more ice. She took out a large slab of side pork and a cigar box filled with big brown eggs. Laying these on the table, she thought, What else do I need? She opened the pantry door and reaching to the back of the top shelf she pulled out a jar of blackberry jam. This was Roy Lee's favorite.

Roy Lee—how she loved her oldest child! He had been born a few months after Al and she had been married. She was almost seventeen at the time. Her contractions had started early one morning after a sleepless night. It was a gray day and a fine mist in the air was turning to snow. Having never experienced contractions before, she hesitated to tell Al in case she was mistaken. The contractions had quit early in the afternoon. The snow kept falling and by nightfall the wind began forming drifts across the driveway in front of the house.

She didn't remember what had awakened her that night. It was either the howling wind or the pang of a muscle contraction. She was instantly aware of Al's loud snoring as he slept in the bed beside her. She lay quietly, listening to the moaning of the old farmhouse as it was being battered by the wind. Suddenly a sharp contraction wrenched her body. She placed her hand over her mouth to muffle the scream. "This must be for real," she thought as beads of perspiration formed on her brow. She sat on the edge of the bed and patiently waited, watching the Big Ben alarm clock on the night stand. She was unable to muffle the scream when another contraction started about three minutes later.

Al opened his eyes; had he heard a scream, or was he only dreaming? Strange, he thought, he didn't feel the warmth of her body next to him. His eyes came into focus and he saw her sitting on the edge of the bed. "Anything wrong, honey?"

"I think the baby's coming," she said between sobs.

He tried to hide the concern and fear in his voice. "Will you be all right while I drive down to the neighbors and use their phone to call the doctor?"

"Hurry," she gasped, bracing for another contraction.

As soon as he had opened the back kitchen door, he knew that it would be impossible for him to get the car out of the driveway. A snowdrift completely covered the doors of the shed where the car was parked. The swirling snow in the darkness of the night cut visibility down to zero at times. He realized that the doctor would never be able to make the twelve miles from Laynard. A wave of fear chilled his body. What if Mary had trouble, he thought, what if the baby died. "God," he said aloud, "what should I do?"

Trying to mask his fear he returned to the bedroom. "It's a regular blizzard out there," he said, nonchalantly. "We'll have to wait until morning before we can get Dr. Kern to come out."

"I can't wait that long," said Mary, between long deep breaths. "Would you go see if Mabel can come? I need someone to help me."

It had taken Al almost two hours to make the half-mile trip to the next-door neighbors and back. He had to struggle through snowdrifts that were almost shoulder high. A couple of times he had lost all sense of direction in the whirling snow and had to wait for a lull in the wind so he could identify the fence posts lining the edge of the road.

Mabel and her husband were sound asleep when Al began pounding on their door. The wind muffled his voice as he cried out their names. Mabel nudged her husband and whispered, "*Was ist das?*"

"*Ich weiss nicht,*" replied her husband as he fumbled for a matchstick in the drawer of the stand beside the bed. Finding one, he struck it on the hardwood floor. It flared in the darkness and as he held it to the wick of a wax candle, a shadowy light filled the room. In their long woolen nightgowns, with the candle held high in front of them, they descended the stairs. They heard the pounding on the front door. When Otto lifted the wooden bolt from the latch, the wind violently blew the door open

"*Was ist los, Herr Al?*" Mabel exclaimed when she saw their snow-covered neighbor standing in the doorway.

"Mary is having a baby and we need someone to help her."

"I vill bee ready in eine minute," she said. "I haben six kinder myself."

Al was amazed at the old German lady as they made their way back down the road. She led the way, making a path through the snowdrifts for him at a pace he could hardly match.

Mary had gotten down the stairs and built a fire in the stove. It seemed as if Al had been gone so long. What if he had gotten lost? She was so relieved when she heard the kitchen door open and heard Mabel's accented voice, "*Hallo, mein Liebchen.*"

Mabel had immediately taken charge. She instructed Al to heat some water and bring all the clean towels he could find. She had picked Mary up in her huge strong arms and carried her to the living room, lying her gently on the over-stuffed flowered sofa. Mabel examined Mary with hands like a skilled surgeon. "It vill be a little longar," she said, "yo jus' squeeze my hand when yo feel der pain, and ve vill have dat little bugger out of der in no time."

Mary was aware of the jabbering of the old German lady, half English and half German. She couldn't understand much of what she was saying but she was mesmerized by the monotonous flow of her words.

Al, sitting impatiently at the kitchen table, heard Mabel say, "Push hard, ist coming!" He tensed as he heard a shrill cry. "It's *ein Junge!*" Mabel triumphantly exclaimed. She brought the wet, wiggling baby boy into the kitchen and said, "He looks jus' like you, Herr Al."

Mary, in the next room, with a smile on her face, had slipped off into sleep.

Two

Mary rolled the dough out evenly on a flour-dusted chopping board. Using the open end of a jelly jar, she cut out rows of biscuits and placed them in a baking tin. The side pork was frying in the cast iron skillet, sending little drops of grease skyrocketing into the air. They should be coming in for breakfast any minute, she thought, as Roy Lee burst through the back door. "Pa is finishing slopping the pigs," he said. "Is there anything you need for me to do?"

"Yes, I will need some firewood for the range since I will be baking this afternoon."

"All right," he said, "I'll get a load in my wagon." What a delightful child, she thought. He was such a sweet, cheerful young man. He had been so much fun to raise. Since he had been her first child she had been able to spend a lot of time with him. She had watched him grow as he nurtured at her breast. She had nursed him through the usual childhood illnesses: whooping cough, chicken pox, scarlet fever, and measles. She had eased his trauma when his dog Shep had been run over by a grain wagon and had died.

Being a mother had been natural for her. She had read Grimms' fairy tales to him at night as he drifted off to sleep. When he was older, they went walking together across the pasture and down through the timber. They would play a game where they would look for things that began with the different letters of the alphabet. How excited he had been the time they were at the end of the alphabet and he had found zucchini growing in the corner of the garden. They would sit on a tree stump in the forest listening to bird calls and then try to mimic them. What a thrill when the bird they were mimicking returned their call. She remembered how they would pick wildflowers and count the petals, then smell the aroma on their fingers.

He was short and stocky in physique, a miniature Al, except for his rosy-red cheeks which he had inherited from his mother.

On his first day of school she had walked down the dirt road with him to the country schoolhouse. She remembered how excited he had been, all dressed up in bib overalls with fresh patches on the knees and his blue, starched work shirt buttoned at the neck. He had two prized possessions tucked under his arm: a wooden cigar box given to him by his grandpa to carry his lunch in, and a thick tablet of ruled paper she had purchased for him at the variety store in Laynard.

He was a good student, almost always getting straight A's on his report cards.

Six huge Duroc sows greedily attacked the slop he poured into the trough. With the morning chores finished, Al turned the five-gallon bucket upside down on the fence post to let it drain, and turned toward the house. The sun had broken free of the horizon and its bright golden rays caused his eyes to squint. As he neared the back porch the mingled aromas of frying side pork and baking biscuits caused a twinge of hunger in his stomach. Some of his farmer friends preferred to eat breakfast before they did morning chores. Al enjoyed the sensations of hunger caused by the early morning activities which whetted his appetite.

"I'm so hungry I could eat a horse and I may just start with you," he said, as he grabbed Mary around the waist. Roy Lee giggled as he stacked the split oak firewood by the range.

"Aren't those other two youngins up yet?" Al asked. There was a shuffling sound at the top of the stairs. A chubby four-year-old boy peeked over the railings. "Is it t-t-time to g-g-get up?" the boy stuttered.

"Good morning, Duck," said Roy Lee. "We thought you were going to sleep all day."

"D-d-don't c-call me that," the boy stammered.

"You shouldn't make fun of your brother, Roy Lee. He can't help it that he's pigeon-toed," scolded Mary.

Al met the four-year-old halfway down the flight of stairs. "Let me give you a piggy-back ride, Gene," Al said, as he lifted the young child high above his head and set him on his shoulders.

He grabbed the chubby legs that barely fit around his neck. Gene squealed in delight, tightly grasping his dad's black hair.

They gathered around the kitchen table. Fried side pork and eggs steamed on a hot platter. A bowl was piled high with biscuits. Still on the range was a double boiler filled with thick oatmeal and plump raisins. Roy Lee noted the jar of blackberry jelly sitting in the middle of the table.

It was his favorite.

When they were seated at the table, they all joined hands. Mary thanked God for all the blessings He had given her family. She prayed that Al and Roy Lee would have a safe trip to the rodeo.

She asked God's blessing on the food before them.

"I hope I can finish breakfast before Jimmy wakes up and I have to nurse him," Mary said.

Al was famished. He piled his plate high with eggs and side pork. He put copious amounts of butter on his biscuits and ate two bowls of oatmeal. "Don't know anybody that's as good a cook as your mother," he said to Roy Lee.

The atmosphere around their kitchen table that morning was peaceful and joyful. Almost like the calm before a storm. Their youngest child, one-year-old Jim, had awakened, just as they finished eating. On her way up the stairs, Mary said to Al, "We need some ice for the icebox before you leave for the rodeo."

"I'll go into town right now and get it," Al replied, "and Roy Lee can help you clean up the breakfast dishes."

Al drove the gray '42 Ford down the country road, deftly missing most of the deeper ruts. His father had given them the car on their fifth wedding anniversary. He didn't like charity, but their old car was broken down and irreparable, so he begrudgingly accepted his father's gift.

Al turned south on highway 65 which led to Laynard. On the left side of the road a small country church came into view with a well-manicured cemetery nearby. Even though he had passed this way many times, a pang of sorrow filled his heart every time he drove by the church.

Today the sadness was especially intense. Under one of the cold tombstones lay their second-born child, Helen.

Helen was born in the early spring just as the fragrance of cherry blossoms filled the air. She was tiny and delicate from the very start, like a china doll with curly black hair and almond eyes. What she lacked in physical stamina she made up for in spirit. When it was feeding time, she would cry at the top of her lungs and wouldn't cease till Mary took her to her breast. When she needed her diaper changed, she would double up her little fists, curl her toes, pucker her face up like a prune and let forth the most horrendous sounds.

Life had been good to them. They had two lovely children, a boy and a girl. The land he farmed had produced bumper crops the first three years they had been married. Mary was very efficient in managing the meager income they had. One night she showed him the coffee can where she had been saving pennies, nickels and dimes. When he asked her what she was going to do with it, she replied, "I'm going to buy you a Sunday suit so we can go to church.

Scarlet fever hit the community and surrounding areas of Laynard when Helen was three years old. All of them except Al had become sick and broke out with a skin rash. Mary became very ill and was near death for about two weeks. Roy Lee and Gene had very light cases and bore the brunt of the disease without any after-effects. Mary recovered, but the disease lingered on in Helen. The doctor had said that it was just taking her body longer to overcome the disease.

Helen's condition continued to worsen and she developed infections in her middle ears. She would scream in intense pain during the mere swallowing of warm broth. A spiking fever began to rack her frail body. Al and Mary had taken turns holding her in their arms during the night, trying to soothe her burning body. She died early one morning around three in Al's arms. The grimace of pain had left her face. She opened her eyes and smiled, telling Al good-by. He had felt the life ebb from her body, free at last of suffering.

They buried Helen on a spring day. Once again the fragrance of cherry blossoms was in the air. On the small tombstone were engraved the words, "A treasure lies here."

Al parked near the rear of the ice house where a ramp went down into the underground storage room. As he descended the stairs he was met with a cool, fresh smell. Block after block of ice, which had been sawed and reaped from the frozen river the winter before, was stacked amid layers of sawdust for insulation. He selected a block which was about fifty pounds in weight.

He picked it up with a pair of ice tongs and carried it to the car. He placed it in the trunk of the car and covered it with a thick woolen blanket. Before he left he placed a dime in the coffee can beside the ramp.

Al drove back down Maple Avenue toward highway 65. He recognized the car in front of him by the red light near the rear window. It was Moe Hendersen, the chief of police in Laynard. He tooted his horn and pulled up alongside the vehicle. Leaning over the passenger side, he said, "Moe, how come you aren't out chasing bandits?"

"Too nice a day. What are you doing in town?"

"Just had to pick up some ice for Mary."

"You going to the rodeo this afternoon?" Moe asked.

"Yes, I'm going to take Roy Lee. He's really excited about going."

"Well, drive careful; the traffic might be pretty heavy since this is the first day and everyone will be wanting to get there early to watch them unload the livestock."

Three

Moe Hendersen had been the chief of police of Laynard going on four years. He enjoyed his job, with its prestige and power. He was considered a good cop by most of the townspeople. Fairness and honesty were his trademarks as he kept order and peace in the small town. He was admired and respected by his peers in the surrounding towns, always ready to share a helping hand or information at their requests. His only weakness, some felt, was that at times he was too lenient, giving a person a second chance when they should have been charged with a misdemeanor.

Moe watched Al turn north on highway 65. A true friend, Moe thought. They had grown up together and had been the best of pals. A special camaraderie had developed between them when they were young boys and had continued into their adulthood. They were opposites. Al was physically well built and had a charming personality. He was outgoing and felt comfortable with anyone, especially the girls. Moe, on the other hand, was very timid, too shy to even catch the eye of a girl, let alone speak to her. He was well over six feet tall and weighed 230 pounds when he was in the twelfth grade. He had a large square face with prominent facial features. His eyes, which were small and beady, seemed out of place below his bushy brows. His nickname was "Ox," but no one ever called him that to his face.

Moe smiled as he remembered the many occasions where Al and he had been in one of the surrounding towns drinking beer in the local tavern. Al, cocky as a bantam rooster, would pick a fight with the biggest customer sitting at the bar, then enlist him to do the fighting. Even though they were good friends, Moe was envious of Al. Somehow he always ended up with the prettiest girl. He was always the center of attention in a crowd, and no one ever made fun of him. But Al always showed Moe respect, treating him as an equal, asking his advice, and fixing him up with blind dates. So, the friendship had flourished. Moe had always had a secret crush on Mary. She was such a wholesome, charming young lady. In his fantasies he had taken her away from Al and they had lived together in bliss as they raised a family. After such daydreaming he felt guilt and shame.

Al and Mary had invited him to supper many times after they were married. He went a few times, but then declined. The nearness of her stirred a lust deep inside him which he couldn't bear.

Moe was married at the age of twenty-eight. His wife was a school teacher, five years his senior. She was tall and thin with a pinched face adorned with round-rimmed reading glasses. She was very prim and proper. Because of her age they wanted to have a child in the very near future. By their reckoning, she became pregnant on their wedding night. Once this became evident, sex became a thing of the past since she didn't want to hurt the baby.

Moe was patient with his wife. He tried to comfort her as she suffered through the period of morning sickness. He treated her with tenderness as he noted the beginning bulge of her stomach. He was ecstatic the first time he felt the baby kick. "If it can kick that hard, it must be a boy," he said with heart-felt happiness.

One morning during her sixth month of pregnancy, his wife had been too sick to get out of bed. The doctor had examined her and said he could see nothing wrong, probably a case of the flu. Two days later she began bleeding and aborted the baby. It had been a boy. After examining her, the doctor had told Moe that his wife would probably never be able to carry a baby to full term. Moe was devastated. His hopes and dreams were shattered, never to become a reality. His wife kept to her bed, becoming a recluse, saying she was being punished by God for her past sins. At first, Moe was angry and cursed God for tempting him with a son, only to withdraw at the last minute, denying Moe the joy and happiness he seemingly had promised him. The anger slowly diminished, and Moe prayed for strength and understanding. To Moe it was a miracle sent forth by the hand of God. The local Baptist minister, Reverend Nye, had knocked on their door one Sunday afternoon. He had told them of his counseling with a family in a nearby town. The teenage daughter of a highly respected family in the community had become pregnant. In an attempt to prevent a scandal, they had sent the girl to live with relatives until after the baby was born. The girl had given birth to a healthy male baby. The parents wanted to put the baby up for adoption without revealing the names of the birth parents.

"In light of your recent loss, I thought you folks might be interested in adopting this young child," said Reverend Nye. "I would highly recommend you to the family if you would be interested."

Moe's heart had leaped with joy. God had answered his prayers. He turned to his wife. "Isn't this great, honey, we can finally have a son."

She looked knowingly at Reverend Nye and said, "Well, you never know what you may be getting. I think we had better talk it over."

"By all means," the minister said. "Could you let me know your decision in a couple of days? The family is anxious to get this matter settled."

After Reverend Nye had left, Moe looked at his wife. Did he really know her, was their relationship what a marriage should be? Wasn't marriage a giving and taking by both people involved? He had never denied her anything. He had listened to her whims and conceded to her every demand.

"Well, what do you think?" he tentatively asked.

"I wouldn't even consider it," she said. "We don't even know who the parents are. We'd be taking the chance of getting a child that had bad blood in its background. Anyhow, how could you expect me to raise someone else's child?"

Moe was repulsed by her words. He had always been very slow to anger, but this brought forth a rage from deep within his soul. Glaring at her, he said, "We are going to adopt this baby, raise it as our own, and be a family. If you don't want to be a part of that family, you can leave my house right now."

She was shocked at his response. This was a side of her husband she had never seen before. Maybe there was something in this mild-mannered man she could learn to respect. "I'll try," she murmured.

Moe remembered the morning they sat patiently waiting in front of the bay windows. This was the day their son was to arrive. They had signed all the paperwork two weeks earlier. The documents stated that they would never attempt to seek out the baby's birth parents. The adoption papers formally gave them guardianship and parental responsibilities for the child. They watched, his wife looking over his shoulder, as Reverend Nye assisted the female social worker out of the car and up the sidewalk. In her arms she held the baby, wrapped in a blue blanket. They didn't wait for the doorbell to ring. Moe met them on the porch, his wife close behind. He had reached for the baby, but his wife gently shoved him aside and gathered the child into her arms.

"Let's see what my son looks like," his wife had said. Moe's heart felt as if it would burst with happiness. Maybe they would be a family after all. They had spent the last week fixing up one of the spare bedrooms for the baby. Moe had painted the walls blue and his wife had made yellow and white frilly curtains to hang on the single window. The room was filled with an array of objects they had anticipated a need for in taking care of a baby. The crib was next to the wall opposite the window. Laying neatly folded on the top sheet was a small knit blanket which Moe's mother had given them. She had knit it for Moe when he was born.

His wife laid the baby tenderly in the crib and pulled the blanket away from his face. Sleepy brown eyes blinked open and a coo escaped the puckered lips. Moe intensely studied the facial features of the child. The face had a squareness to it and there were high cheekbones with a strong chin and prominent nose. "He looks like me," Moe exclaimed.

"He sure does," said his wife, "and isn't he big for only being four weeks old?"

They named him Moe Chester Hendersen, Jr.

Moe parked the police car in the reserved space behind the city hall. Instead of taking the shortcut to his office through the side door, he opted to walk around to the front of the building and enter by the front door. His uniform was fitting tighter every day; it seemed like either it had shrunk or he was adding pounds to an already overweight body. He had guessed it was the latter and knew the lack of physical activity was part of the reason. The extra steps around to the front of the building weren't many, but every little bit helped.

Entering his office, he was greeted by a sexy voice. "Good morning, Chief." Louise was a nineteen-year-old who worked part-time for him answering the telephone while he was on patrol. She was sitting in his office chair with her legs crossed, reading a comic book. Her lower jaw was moving in a rhythmical manner as she popped air pockets in a large wad of bubble gum. She was clad in skin-tight shorts and a low-cut blouse. He smiled to himself and thought, She looks like a heifer in heat chewing her cud.

"Any phone calls yet this morning?" he asked.

"Yes, a Mr. Ed Welsh from the rodeo committee wants you to call him this morning."

Moe looked at his watch. It read 9:10 A.M.

He wondered what Ed Welsh wanted this early in the morning, probably some stupid question like, How's the rodeo traffic down your way? He really didn't care much for Mr. Welsh, he had become so damn patronizing since he had been named chairman of the rodeo board. He had been successful, though, in getting the National Rodeo Association to select Carville as a sight to build a fairgrounds where rodeo competition could take place. This would be the sixth consecutive year that the event had taken place. It had been a boon for the small towns of Laynard and Carville, the county seat. Visitors came from all over the country to attend the performances which occurred daily for five days. Every hotel room and boarding house would be filled for miles around and cash registers would ring up sales of souvenirs. The churches in the two communities had food concession on the fairgrounds, and many of them made enough profit on their food sales to completely cover their yearly budgets. The stores just across the state line five miles south of Laynard did a landslide business selling liquor and beer since the rodeo was in a dry county.

"Do you have his phone number?"

"Sure do, Chief," she said, picking up a piece of scratch paper from his desk. "I'll get him on the phone for you."

Moe immediately recognized the voice on the other end of the line by the nasal twang. "What's up, Ed?"

"How's the good chief of police this morning?" came the whiny voice over the phone.

"Get on with it," Moe thought. "Fine," he answered, "looks like it's going to be a hot one today."

"Say, I was wondering if you had ever thought about setting up a roadblock south of Laynard on highway 65 and searching for illegal alcohol that people are bringing across the state line? It would probably help keep some of the riff-raff out of our fair city of Carville during the rodeo."

Riff-raff, shit, thought Moe. Ed Welsh was one of the biggest alcoholics in the county. It was even said that he sold bootleg alcohol out of the basement of his home. "I'll see if I have time," Moe said, "but you gotta realize that I have to patrol the whole southwest sector of the county."

Moe let the receiver slam back down on the phone. What a waste of time, he thought. If people wanted to bring liquor across the state line, they'd do it. Roadblocks wouldn't be a deterrent.

Louise stood up and leaned over, resting her elbows on the top of his desk. Her loose-fitting blouse gave him a full view of her braless breasts. If I was a few years younger I'd make her regret that, he thought.

"Anything else you need?" she asked. "Remember I asked for this afternoon off."

"Oh, yes, I remember. Going to the rodeo?"

"Yes," she lied. She was actually going to spend the afternoon with her new lover. Joe had called her the week before to see if she could secretly meet him this afternoon.

Four

Panic gripped his body as Joe awoke from a deep sleep. The nightmare had reoccurred. He couldn't remember when he first had it but it was sometime after his mother had died. Early on it had plagued him periodically every two or three weeks, but recently he hadn't experienced it for over a year. In an awakened state the visual images remained, causing tremors of fear to rack his body. He was lying on his back, tied to the framework of a metal cot. High above him, hanging in folds from the ceiling, was a gigantic spider web. Descending directly above his face, on a single strand of web was a large black spider. As it came close to his face, he could see the poison dripping from its proboscis and its long, hairy antennae moving menacingly in space. As it came closer one could see the many facets of its eyes, each containing a small evil black pupil. Joe turned on the shower, hoping to wash away the images of the nightmare. The warm rivulets of water gently massaged his muscular back. His body relaxed and he luxuriated in the heavy dampness of the shower stall. The nightmare was shoved back into his subconscious level, replaced by thoughts of Louise in his conscious mind. He could see her nude breasts, young and curved. He could feel their supple firmness. Lust welled up in his groin and desire rushed through his veins. He was going to make love to her again today.

Joe had experienced a troubled childhood. His father had been sent to prison when Joe was four years old. He had stabbed a man during a drunken brawl and the man had died. His mother, left alone to raise a young child, had turned to prostitution. There was a steady stream of strangers visiting their two-bedroom bungalow at night. Some of them would ignore him. Some would call him "Sonny" or "Boy." Usually there was only one male visitor at a time but on occasion there were two. One evening a male and a female spent the night with his mother.

He had vivid memories of lying awake in his bed at night listening to the sounds in his mother's bedroom across the hall. The moaning and the panting accompanied by the squeaking of the bedsprings would go on for hours. At times it would sound like a lair of animals fighting for a morsel of food. He would bury his head in his pillow trying to muffle the sound. When the noise stopped he could hear his mother's soft sobbing. He couldn't comprehend what was happening but he sensed that it was evil and in some way it made him feel guilty.

He remembered the first time one of the kids on the playground called his mother a whore. Innocently he had asked, "What's that?"

"She screws men for money," the boy replied. Joe still didn't quite understand, but anger rose up inside him and he had doubled the boy over with a blow to the stomach and then crushed his nose with an uppercut. That was the last time anyone called his mother a whore to his face.

By the time he was ten years old, he was working a part-time job after school and on Saturdays, unloading freight cars at the train yards. The work was hard and demanding, lifting heavy boxes and crates. His muscles grew and his body matured quickly, making him look older than his classmates. He was a good student, excelling beyond his classmates in almost all of his subjects. He was well-liked by his teachers. They predicted he would go places in the world even with his unsavory family background.

His mother died suddenly one morning from a stroke. He was fourteen years old at the time. His heart was heavy with grief. It had happened so quickly that he didn't have time to tell her he loved her. He cried himself to sleep that night. There were no sounds in the bedroom across the hall.

A letter had come to the apartment addressed to his mother the week after she had died. The return address indicated that it was from the state parole board. It must be something concerning his father, he had thought. It had been nine years since his father had sent his last letter. Joe tore the letter open. It stated that his father would be paroled from prison on May 10, after serving the mandatory ten years for the conviction of second degree murder.

On May 10, he had skipped school and stayed all day in the apartment, hoping the phone would ring. It never did. His father had made no attempt to contact him. He was fourteen years old with no family and no one to call his own. He decided that the world was a cruel place to live.

Joe stepped out of the shower and reached for the terry cloth towel which hung neatly folded on the towel rack. He stood in front of the mirror admiring his physique as he vigorously dried his hair. He caught the reflection of his wife Rosie in the mirror. She was still in bed, sprawled out on top of the bedspread. Her baby-doll pajamas failed to hide the fat dimples on her ample thighs. Her once long, curly red hair now hung short and straight with streaks of gray. It had been the second marriage for both of them.

Joe had quit school shortly after his mother had died. He worked various odd jobs and spent most of his evenings with friends drinking bootleg liquor purchased across the state line. On one such occasion, in a state of drunkenness, he had made love to Amanda, the fifteen-year-old daughter of one of the town's prominent businessmen. She had become pregnant. Faced with the physical and legal threats of her father, he had consented to marry her. They were forced to live with her parents since neither of them had any financial means. They converted the dark, damp basement of her parents' home into a makeshift apartment. They had a hot plate to heat their meals on and a utility sink under the stairway. There were no toilet facilities so they had to use the ones on the first floor. Amanda was a very timid young girl prone to crying at even the most insignificant disagreement. He stayed away from the house as much as he could, working long hours and drinking with his friends. His father-in-law constantly badgered him, calling him a no-good, worthless bastard. He let it be known in the community that his daughter deserved more than this shiftless hooligan. Joe bit his lower lip and tried to keep peace in the family.

When the baby, a strapping boy, was born, Joe spent more time at home. He was intrigued with this miniature human being, so tiny and helpless, yet so demanding. He helped bathe the child and change his diapers. He would hold the child in his arms in the evenings and rock him to sleep. He began to hope that a grandson would soften the relationship between him and his father-in-law. The relationship, however, got worse. He was accused of being an unfit father who couldn't even support his own child. His wife gave him no support. She cowered whenever she was in the same room with her father, afraid to defend Joe.

Joe started spending more time with his friends. He started drinking more and sometimes never came home at night, which fueled more insults from his father-in-law. He had met Rosie one Saturday night at a dance in a neighboring town.

She had asked him to dance when the bandleader had announced it was lady's choice. She looked to be in her mid-twenties, probably seven or eight years his senior. She had long, curly red hair and large, sensuous lips enlarged with bright coral lipstick. A black slit skirt fit tightly around the curves of her full, rounded hips. Even without a bra, she carried her breasts high and the brown nipples came dangerously close to penetrating the loose knit sweater she wore. She had hugged her body close to his as they danced, and he could smell a fragrance in her hair as she laid her head on his chest. They danced many dances together that night.

A week later Joe had returned to the same dance hall. In the back of his mind lingered a desire to see her again. She was there too, hoping to see him again. She gave him an inviting look when their eyes met. They danced most of the dances together that evening and later on he asked to take her home. They parked behind an abandoned feed store south of town. Joe remembered how she had teased him, placing her hand on his thigh, then pulling away as he fumbled for her breasts. She had turned her head when he had first tried to kiss her, then offered him her lips and darted her tongue into his mouth. Passion swelled up in his body to the point of panic. Finally she slipped off her sweater and pulled his head down to her brown nipples.

Joe was consumed with Rosie's lovemaking. They had tried to keep their relationship secret, but it soon became public. When the knowledge reached his father-in-law, the roof caved in. With a shotgun in hand, he had intercepted Joe one night on the front porch as he came home from work. He threatened to shoot Joe if he ever set foot in his house again.

Rosie awoke from a strange dream; she was a little girl again and this evil-looking man was forcing her to touch his private parts. She shuddered and opened her eyes. Through the bathroom door she could see Joe. He was completely naked except for the towel draped around his shoulders. He still looked as young as that eighteen-year-old boy she had married sixteen years ago. She had been twenty-five at the time. A wave of pleasure swept across her body as she remembered their lovemaking during those early years.

Joe had wanted to have children, but as time went by it became obvious that they would remain childless. Their lovemaking began to wane and became a necessary ritual that she had to instigate. Time had not been kind to her body. Her once firm, supple body was now on the verge of obesity.

A cough racked her body, causing her to gasp for breath. She reached for the pack of cigarettes on the small table beside the bed. The end of the cigarette glowed brightly as she inhaled. The hot smoke irritated her lungs, causing a choking sensation. She tried to clear the phlegm from her throat but couldn't dislodge the viscid secretions.

"When are you going to see a doctor about that damn cough?" asked Joe from the bathroom.

"It's just a summer cold," she replied between gasps.

The mirror reflected the look of disgust on Joe's face. Let's not start the day off like this, she thought. "How come you're up so early showering? You want to come back to bed and I'll make love to you?"

He turned and glared at her. "Don't you remember anything I tell you? Two weeks ago I informed you that I was taking my son to the rodeo today." It was a perfect plan. He would pick up his son, take him to the rodeo and tell him that he had to meet someone about a job. While the rodeo performance was taking place, he would drive to Laynard and spend the afternoon secretly making love to Louise. He had called her to be sure she could get time off from her job in the police chief's office. Louise had been taking orders at a drive-in cafe when he first met her. "What have you got that's hot," he said, as she pulled the pencil from behind her ear to take his order. "I have anything you want, but it may be too hot for you," she had replied, looking him straight in the eye.

"How about picking it up later?"

"Sure," she said. "I close tonight, I'll be getting off around midnight."

That night he had made love to her as she sat on the counter in the darkened cafe. That had been almost three weeks ago, and he couldn't wait to taste the sweetness of her lips again.

Rosie watched Joe pull the tight-fitting Levis up over his hips, tuck in his cowboy shirt, and then button the waistband. He never wore a belt. He jokingly told his friend that he didn't want anything slowing him down when he was taking his pants off. Rosie looked at him and wondered if he was messing around with another woman. She could hardly stand the thought of him in bed with someone else. She really couldn't blame him though, if he was having an affair. She felt as though she had never fully satisfied his sexual needs, that there had always been something missing in their relationship.

Well, I'll get all fixed up today, she thought, and when he comes home from the rodeo tonight, I'll make love to him like I used to.

Five

Roy Lee was waiting by the front-yard gate when Al returned with the ice. At Mary's insistence he had washed his hair and put on clean bib overalls and a fresh, starched work shirt. "I got all the work done for Mom," he said.

"Okay, we'll leave as soon as I get the ice in the house." By leaving now they would get to Carville by midmorning, and maybe arrive before the heavy traffic, Al thought. That would give them time to browse around the fairgrounds before the performance started.

"Meet anybody in town that you knew?" Mary asked as Al carried the dripping ice across the kitchen and placed it in the wooden ice box.

"Just Moe, but I didn't talk to him very long." A warm blush reddened Mary's cheeks. She quickly turned lest Al notice. She had always had a special feeling for Moe. He was such a kind and gentle person. She could feel an attraction between them whenever they were in each other's presence. She was sure that Moe sensed this too. He had never indicated it by words or actions, but she could see it in his eyes.

Mary stood on the front porch with the baby Jim in her arms and Gene standing by her side. She waved good-by to Al and Roy Lee as they pulled out of the driveway. She watched until the car disappeared in a wake of trailing dust. As she turned, a foreboding aura encompassed her, the same sensation she remembered having the day before Helen had died.

Memories of her daughter came flooding back to her. She remembered standing beside the casket in the little country cemetery, unable to forgive God for taking her precious belonging. It had taken a long time for the pain to ease. Slowly time acted as a healing balm, easing her grief, and life went on. When she felt life stirring within her womb again she remembered the words of the minister at the funeral: "The Lord giveth and the Lord taketh away." Maybe God would give her another daughter. She prayed that he would.

The baby in her arms began to fuss. "Is it time to nurse you again?" she asked. She was going to be busy the rest of the day. A belated birthday supper for Roy Lee was in the making. She had planned all of his favorite foods. Fried chicken, corn on the cob, mashed potatoes and gravy, and apple pie were all on the menu.

Roy Lee watched out the back window of the car until his mother and brothers disappeared from sight in the dust. "I wish Mom could have come with us," he said.

"She really didn't think she would enjoy it," Al said, knowing they couldn't afford the extra ticket and not wanting to place the burden of taking care of the two younger children on his parents. "Maybe we can all go together next year."

As they approached highway 65, there was an old lady leaning on a hoe in a garden patch near the dirt road they were on. When she saw them she frantically motioned them to stop.

"There's Mabel," Al said. "We had better stop and say hello to her."

Mabel loved Roy Lee as if he were one of her own. She had brought him into the world on that cold winter night over nine years ago. She had bathed him, wrapped him in a blanket and laid him in his mother's arms. His young mother had often asked her for advice in the raising of the child. She had been an excellent coach for Mary during her early years of motherhood. When scarlet fever struck Al's family, she had ignored the danger to her own health and well-being, spending two weeks in their home taking care of the children as Mary lay ill in bed.

"*Guten Morgen, mein Leib*," she said, as she approached the passenger side of the car. Leaning through the window, she gave him an enormous hug. Roy Lee excitedly told her about his late birthday present, going to the rodeo with his father.

"*Das ist gut*," she exclaimed and made them promise to stop on their way home and she'd have a surprise for him. He knew it would be her special fudge brownies.

Al turned north on highway 65. It was a typical summer day. A few fluffy clouds lolled in the sky, occasionally blocking out the direct rays of the sun. The humidity was high. The breeze coming through the open windows of the car cooled the small beads of sweat on their foreheads. Fields of green-tasseled corn grew close to the edge of the road. They rode in silence, each in deep thought with visual images of the coming afternoon. As they finessed a tight S curve on the old two-lane highway, the traffic intensified ahead of them.

"Looks like a lot of people had the same idea we did," Al commented as he gently tapped the brakes.

"I wish we'd hurry up and get there," was Roy Lee's impatient reply.

As they entered the parking lot, traffic slowed to a snail-like bumper-to-bumper pace. Men with swinging arms directed them down long rows of cars to a parking space. Roy Lee had his door opened before the car came to a full stop. He tentatively reached in the back seat for his rain poncho, but looking up into the clear blue sky decided not to take it. There was excitement in the air. Somewhere a band played music. Tractors moaned under heavy loads of hay and straw. Human voices directed animals through long lanes of fences to the arena pens.

The carnival midway, adjacent to the parking lot, was busy with activities. Carnies were putting up tents, displaying their wares. Shills, standing on little wooden platforms, enticed bystanders to try their luck at games of chance. The brassy notes of a pipe organ located the carousel with its brightly painted wooden horses.

Roy Lee was filled with awe and excitement at the sights and activity around him. Behind one of the tents, in a grassy spot, a troupe of midgets were practicing their tumbling act. What funny-looking people, he thought. They were so small, yet had large heads and hands, making them look like grown-ups. He smiled at their antics, double flips in the air, landing on their hands, and then freezing in a handstand. He saw clowns dressed in bright-colored clothing; their faces were painted, some happy, some sad.

They passed a makeshift stage where dogs were performing tricks. The small dogs were dressed up as people and walked on their hind legs. Two of them actually danced together to the music blaring from a lone speaker attached to a nearby light post. At the top of a billboard, in large red letters, were written the words, WONDERS OF THE WORLD. Below were pictures of a two-headed snake, a three-legged calf, a fat lady, and a man whose hands were shaped like a bird's foot.

Workmen were hastily assembling a large Ferris wheel. The iron seats squeaked and swung lazily as it rotated. A long black belt attached to a steam engine turned the gigantic wheel. "Dad, have you ever ridden in one of those?" Roy Lee asked. "No, and I don't think I ever want to. Let's walk down to the barns and see if we can meet some of the cowboys."

In the field next to the animal barns was an array of trailers, pick-ups with attached campers, and repainted school buses.

This was home for the cowboys on the rodeo circuit. They ate their meals at a common chuck wagon and would gather around campfires at night telling stories about their life in the rodeo.

"How would you like a hat like that?" Al said as they approached the area where the campfire had been the night before.

Roy Lee noted the distinguished attire of the cowboys. They all wore big ten-gallon hats, some with floppy brims, others with the brims curved stiffly upward on the sides. Their shirts were colorful and bright, and most of them had ornate designs on the boots. Their conversation was slow and gentle, words flowing together with their southern drawl. All of the cowboys seemed to be busy. One was twirling a rope with a loop at one end, another was polishing a saddle. They walked up to one who was braiding a lead rope for a halter.

"Howdy," said Al. "You getting ready for the competition this afternoon?"

A smiling young face appeared under the brim of the ten-gallon hat. "I suppose so; are you folks planning on going to the performance?"

"Yes, this here is my son Roy Lee. He turned nine years old earlier this year so I promised him I'd bring him to the rodeo."

"Well, I'm going to be riding Old Sugar Foot, the meanest Brahma bull in the country, so cheer for me when you see #32 come out of the chute." The cowboy told them how he had grown up on a ranch in western Montana. Times had been so hard there that he decided to try his hand at the rodeo business. He had ridden his first bull three years ago, in Casper, Wyoming, at the age of fifteen. "So you are celebrating your birthday today," the cowboy said. "Well, I'd like to give you a present." He reached over to his saddlebag and pulled out a photograph. Turning it over, he wrote on the back, "To my friend, Roy Lee, from Tex Oakes."

Roy Lee turned the picture over and saw a huge Brahma bull with its back arched high. Riding the bull, with his ten-gallon hat in his free hand, was the cowboy Tex. "Thank you,"

Roy Lee said, as he carefully placed it in the pocket of his work shirt and securely buttoned down the flap.

Bidding the cowboy good-by, they retraced their steps back to the midway. The crowd had intensified. Lines of people had formed, waiting to get into the different side shows. There was an especially long line of men in front of a tent that had a sign saying, "Burlesque: Direct from Paris." Roy Lee thought the scantily clad lady taking tickets was very pretty. As they came to the end of the midway the air was filled with delicious aromas of food being cooked. Food concession stands were clustered around the shade of a grove of oak trees. Open-faced grills held beds of steaming hot-dogs. Cooks with sweat showing on the aprons flipped crackling hamburgers in large frying pans. Long rows of cups filled with black coffee rapidly disappeared from the counters. Rack after rack of home-baked pies of every imaginable flavor filled the shelves on the sides of the stands. Whole chickens roasted above beds of charcoal and vats of pork ribs cooked in bubbling barbecue sauce. The visions of food stimulated pangs of hunger and the aroma in the air caused their saliva to flow. They found two empty seats at the stand operated by the Laynard Methodist Church. Roy Lee ordered two pieces of chicken, an apple tart, and a bottle of root beer. Al ordered ribs, two slices of homemade bread with orange marmalade, and black coffee. They ate in silence, each relishing the taste of the food. After they had finished, Al pulled out a tin of Prince Albert tobacco and a sheer piece of paper and rolled a cigarette. He lit it, inhaled deeply, and contentedly finished his coffee.

When they left the concession stand they headed toward the grandstand, which enclosed the north end of the arena. There were no lines forming yet at the main entrance; a few people had filtered into the bleachers at the south end of the arena. "We got some time to kill," Al said. "We might as well go over and look at the animals in the arena pens."

Behind the grandstand was the holding area for the animals taking part in the rodeo for the day. It was a checkerboard arrangement of pens formed with wooden fences. In the various pens were small calves which were used for roping, large steers used in the bulldogging events, shaggy broncos which had been bred for bucking, and in one reinforced enclosure were the fierce Brahma bulls. There also were sleek Quarter horses tethered to the wood railings. They were highly groomed with long manes and polished hooves and wore ornate saddles.

The first animals Roy Lee noted when they approached the pens were the Brahma bulls. He peered through the rail fence. He had never seen one up close before. The one nearest to him was pawing the ground with one of its forelegs, throwing dirt high over its back. Its curved pointed horns glistened in the sunlight. Sensing the presence of a human being, it turned its massive head to look at the young boy peering though the railing. It stared at Roy Lee through angry eyes, then lifted its head and snorted loudly, causing mucus to drip from its nostrils. Roy Lee shuddered; he wondered if that was Old Sugar Foot.

Moe Hendersen, chief of police, watched the accented swaying of the hips in the tight pair of shorts as Louise left his office. "I wonder who the lucky guy is that's getting in her pants?" he thought.

An antique fan, sitting on the floor about five feet from his chair, droned incessantly. Its maximum output was unable to stir the loose leaves of paper lying neatly on his desk. Moe leaned forward in his chair and picked up the morning mail which Louise had placed in the incoming mail file. He sorted out the important letters from the junk mail and mused, "Eighteen pieces of trash and three keepers." Piece by piece, he flipped the unopened junk letters, sailing them toward a wastepaper can about six feet from his desk. When he had gone through the pile he noted all but one piece had made it into the can. "Not a bad average," he thought.

Moe looked at the large tri-state map covering most of one wall of his office. There was a small flag sticking in the dot that was labeled Laynard. Laynard, population 1,250, was the last town in the corner of the state. He had spent all his life in Laynard. His father and mother owned and worked in the small variety store on Main and First Street. Growing up, he had spent his late afternoons and weekends stocking the various merchandise in shelves that lined the sides of the store. When he finished high school he continued working in the store. Everyone in Laynard, including his parents, assumed he would take over the business from his parents. When he was twenty-five years old, a friend of his father's, the chief of police of Carville, offered him a job as custodian at the county jailhouse. Carville was the county seat and was about thirty miles north on highway 65. He had found the work interesting and quickly made friends with the chief and his assistant. They offered to let him ride on patrols. He was thrilled with the sensations of the high speed chase, the piercing whine of the siren, and the blinking red cherry on top of the patrol car. He would watch and listen closely as the chief interrogated a suspect. He learned the lingo and actively participated in the daily operations of the office. He could hardly manage on the salary that he was paid but he enjoyed the experiences so much. Four years passed before the dream opportunity arose.

The city council of the town of Laynard had voted to establish a position of chief of police. Even though he had no formal training, the council voted unanimously to offer him the job.

The wooden octagonal clock chimed the half hour. "Eleven thirty already," Moe noted, "should be out patrolling, the traffic is probably picking up." He dialed the phone and waited for the familiar voice of his wife. "Hello, honey, Louise took the afternoon off and I was wondering if you wanted to come down to the office and have lunch with me and then cover the phone calls for a couple of hours? Moe Junior could take his nap on the cot I have in the back room."

"I'd love to, and I'm sure your son will be delighted."

"Okay, I'll pick up some hamburgers and fries and meet you down here in about fifteen minutes."

Moe waited patiently in the patrol car for the carhop to

bring him his order. He thought about the pleasant turn his life had taken since the adoption of Moe Jr. His wife had taken to motherhood with a passion. The bonds of love had grown strongly between her and the child from the very beginning. She had nurtured the child as if it was her very own. At first she had referred to the child as "my baby." A subtle change took place after the first month; she begin referring to the child as "our baby." She blossomed as time went by, coming out of her reclusive shell. She had joined a sewing club and participated in the Ladies Aid group at the Methodist Church. An excellent piano player, she began offering music lessons to children in the community.

They were waiting for him when he returned to the office. Moe Jr., going on five years of age, spied the patrol car pulling into the reserved parking space. "Daddy, Daddy, can I turn on the siren?" he pleaded, as his chubby legs carried him running down the sidewalk.

Moe caught the boy just as he tripped on a crack in the curb. "How are you, Tiger?" he said, tossing the boy high into the air over his head.

"Daddy, I want to hear the siren."

"Not now," his father said, "we might scare someone. Besides we got these burgers to eat."

They spread napkins out on top of his desk and unwrapped their hamburgers, which were stacked high with pickles, tomatoes, and lettuce, and dripping with ketchup and mayonnaise. They ate, talking above the drone of the floor fan.

"If Ed Welsh calls this afternoon, tell him I made a trip down to the state line to check things out," Moe said to his wife. "And don't let Junior make too much of a mess around here."

Moe leaned down to give his wife a peck on the forehead. She raised her head to meet his lips with hers. He squeezed her shoulder as the kiss lingered. "Be careful, honey," she said. The nagging fear of something happening to her husband lingered in her mind whenever he was out patrolling. In the evening when he was gone she would have visions of high-speed chases where he would lose control of the patrol car and go careening off a cliff. Even though she knew he was cautious and careful, accidents did happen.

Moe turned south on highway 65. The oncoming traffic was heavy, almost bumper-to-bumper, and there was the expected impatient honking of horns. There were no cars in sight in his lane. He crossed the state line and noted that several liquor stores were doing a brisk business. "Sure would save a lot of problems if our state would go back to legalizing the sale of alcohol," he thought. "All that money going out of the state." He made a U-turn and headed back. Even though the traffic was heavy, it was flowing smoothly. "It would create chaos to set up a road block to check for illegal possession of alcohol," he decided. "It would back up the traffic for miles."

Staying on highway 65, he continued north past Laynard. Mary came to his mind. He hadn't seen her for so long. He wondered how obvious it would be if he dropped in to see her. Al would have left by now to take his son to the rodeo. He pulled out of the traffic, making a left-hand turn onto the country road. A feeling of culpability stole over him but it didn't deter him from continuing down the road.

Mary was rolling out the crust for an apple pie when she saw the squad car pull up the drive. She quickly dusted the flour from her hands and straightened her house dress. Gene was upstairs playing with his toys and Jimmy was asleep in his crib.

Mary brushed back the wisp of hair hanging down on her forehead as she walked out the front door. "Moe Hendersen," she said. "I haven't seen you for months; where have you been keeping yourself?"

"Oh, I've been around, keeping the peace in Laynard," he said, grinning. "I saw Al this morning and he said he was taking Roy Lee to the rodeo this afternoon. I was just driving by and thought I'd drop in to see if you were okay."

They faced each other, about an arm's length apart, making small talk about the weather, neither hearing what the other said. They looked deep into each other's eyes and saw desire. Both of them wanted to reach out and touch the other, but were afraid of the passion that would be unleashed.

Moe was the first to avert his eyes; he realized he was close to doing something that could ruin both of their lives.

Six

Rosie reached for the chiming telephone. "Hello, Tad. Your dad's right here," she said, and handed the phone to Joe. She was happy that Joe had maintained a relationship with his sixteen-year-old son from his first marriage. After his divorce his previous father-in-law had forbidden Joe to have any contact with his son, threatening to physically harm him if he tried. Joe had made repeated attempts to contact his wife with no success. He had finally gone to court and obtained visitation rights and later was allowed to take the child on weekends. The relationship between father and son had grown quite strong. The child related to Joe and rebelled against his grandfather, who was the other dominant male in his life. Rosie enjoyed having the stepson in her home. It had made her feel less guilty when she was unable to give Joe a son of their own.

"Hi, kid," Joe said into the receiver. "Yes, I'll pick you up in about an hour. Tell your mother I'll get you back in time for supper." Tad's mother had never remarried. They still lived in her father's house. Her mother had died but the old man, bedridden, was still alive. She nursed him twenty-four hours a day. Her only happiness in life was her son. She was so proud of him. He had just turned sixteen years old and was looking more like his father every day.

"How come you're going to pick Tad up so early?" Rosie said as Joe hung up the receiver.

"I thought I told you; I'm going to drop him off early at the rodeo. Then I have to meet a client who wants to buy some insurance, but I should get done in time to get to see most of the performance with Tad."

A hint of guilt passed through Joe's mind as he lied. He had lied to her so often that the sensation didn't even register, and his thoughts turned to Louise. He would be able to meet her at an abandoned log cabin near Laynard, make love to her, and still make it back to see most of the rodeo performance with his son.

Louise walked rapidly as she left the chief's office, heading for her parent's house six blocks north on Main Street. She wanted to have plenty of time to take a bath and dry her hair before she met Joe at the little log cabin about half a mile west on an abandoned road.

Her stepfather was sitting in an antique, dilapidated leather recliner in the front room as she entered the house. He was reading from an old earmarked Bible, his round-rimmed glasses perched precariously on the end of his large nose. What a pig, she thought.

Her father had been a blacksmith and leather tanner in a neighboring town. He had been a swarthy man, big and strong, and could put the devil on the run with his cursing. He would come home at night dirty and sweaty from his work, reeking with the smell of burning charcoal and moldy leather. Her mother was a petite, shy, yet proper woman. Louise had come to their bedroom door late one night when she was four years old. She saw her father, still covered with dirt and grime, repeatedly forcing himself into her mother. She pulled back in horror, and believed all men were animals. When she was six years old, her mother had taken her to a revival meeting held in a large tent at the city park. The itinerant preacher had given a sermon on sin. He explained that if we live in proximity to sin the sin would become part of us, therefore it was critical that we remove ourselves from the presence of sin.

"Enter our bodies!" the minister had screamed as he began to sway in mystical rhythm. "Drive out Satan and cleanse our bodies of sin!" His chanting whipped the small congregation into a glorified frenzy. People began to dance in the aisles, lifting their arms upward, and chanting in strange voices. Lunging and jerking, they yelled at God. Children looked up toward heaven in holy terror.

Her mother had felt the rapture, and when the minister had invited those that desired to accept God to come forth, she responded. Louise sensed a sinister tone in the way the minister had laid his hands on her mother and her. They attended the revival meeting every night for the next six days. On the last night they had stayed after the service was over. The minister had talked to her mother in low, convincing tones. Louise had heard him say, "The only way you can be saved from damnation is to get away from the presence of sin." The next morning her mother had packed two suitcases and they had left town, sitting with the itinerant minister in the cab of his pick-up with the large tent folded up in the back.

They had traveled the back roads, stopping at small farming communities and setting up the tent. The minister would preach fire-and-brimstone sermons, urging the people that the only way the world could be saved was if they filled the collection plates so he could keep fighting the fight against Satan. On some occasions he was booed, and they would pack up over night and leave in the cover of darkness. Usually, though, they would collect enough money to buy the food they needed and gas for the pick-up to take them to the next town.

One afternoon while her mother was shopping, she was playing with her rag doll in the back of the tent. The minister was sitting at a makeshift desk preparing his sermon for the evening meeting. He called her over to his side. "Louise, if you want to be saved you have to do what God tells you to do," he said.

"What's that?" she had innocently asked. "Come sit on my lap," he said. As she came near he picked her up and set her firmly between his legs. As he pressed her firmly against his thighs she could feel the hardness under her. She felt him shudder, then he shoved her off his lap.

"You're an evil girl," he said. "You must ask God to forgive you. If you ever tell anyone that you sit on my lap, Satan will take your soul away to hell."

The next day, when her mother was not around, he had come up behind her, picked her up, and sat down in his chair, holding her tightly on his lap, and said, "God will forgive you if you don't tell anyone." This became a regular ritual between them until her mother had caught them when she was about ten years old. He had never attempted it again, but she was constantly aware of the lust in his perverted eyes.

Her father had died when she was twelve years old. The minister, not wanting to live in a state of sin, offered to marry her mother. "God took your husband to free you from sin," he had told her mother, "and has instructed me to marry you so you may be saved." Her mother had accepted it as God's will.

They had traveled to the small town of Laynard and set up the revival tent. The crowd had responded favorably to her stepfather's preaching. A deacon at one of the churches, which had recently lost its pastor, approached him and offered him the pulpit in the local church. Tired of the vigor of traveling and never knowing if the collection plates would yield enough for them to live on, he had accepted the position. That had been six years ago. Louise had been ecstatic. She could finally make some friends and go to a real school instead of learning the lessons her mother had prepared for her. Also, she would never have to help put up that musty, foul-smelling tent again.

In her early teens Louise had been aware that men were attracted to her. She enjoyed the attention and as she grew older encouraged them to flirt with her. At the age of fourteen, she had let a young man make a fumbling attempt to make love to her. She soon found that older men were more adept at fulfilling her physical needs. That's why she had been so attracted to Joe.

"Where's Mom?" she asked her stepfather as she closed the door.

"She's down at the church doing the books. Why are you home so early? I thought you were working today at the chief's office."

"I'm going to meet a friend," she said.

"I hope you are going to change your clothes, those shorts you have on are the tools of the Devil. You should be ashamed of yourself parading around in public like that, trying to tempt the weakness of men. God's wrath will surely fall upon you. The Good Book says that those who are evil will suffer the fires of hell for all eternity."

"Piss on the book," she said. She went into the kitchen and searched the icebox for something to eat. Finding nothing, she opened the cupboard door and took out the peanut butter and made a sandwich. She washed it down with a glass of milk, then went down the stairs to the basement where their only shower was located. Stripping down completely, she dropped her clothes in the hamper. There were no bath towels in the closet. She dug her silk panties out of the hamper, slipped them up around her slim waist, and went back up the stairs to get a towel from the hall closet. When she walked through the front room she saw the desire in her stepfather's hawkish eyes. His stare was fixed on the dark shadow of the pubic hair evident under her silk panties.

"Want me to sit on your lap?" she sneered.

"You bitch," he said, and lowered his eyes.

Meanwhile, Joe was dropping his son off at the entrance gate to the rodeo. He had lied to him about the supposed client he had to meet. "I'll meet you in the grandstand later on," Joe said, "but if our wires get crossed, I'll meet you here at the gate after the performance is over."

Joe turned south on highway 65. He had to pick up some liquor at the state line before he met Louise. She had told him that she liked rum and Coke. He usually drank beer, but today he'd get a bottle of hard liquor and mix it with 7-Up. He faced a steady line of oncoming traffic, but the lane ahead of him was void of cars.

The trip seemed longer than usual to Joe. His mind turned to his father. No matter how hard he tried he could never develop a mental image of him in his mind. His mother told him that he had his father's facial features. He had only been four years old the last time he had seen his father. That had been the day before he left the county jail and was transferred to the state prison farm. He remembered how he would lie when his playmates asked him where his father was. He would tell them that his daddy was a sailor on a big sailing ship and that he was somewhere out in the ocean heading for China. He had even begun to believe this. He fantasized standing at the helm with his father, directing a ship through an angry sea, yelling out orders to the crew to trim the sails.

After that had come anger. He cursed his father for leaving him and his mother alone. He would never forgive him for not being there when he needed a father. Later the anger left and only curiosity remained. He wondered if his father was still alive. Where did he live? Did he have any children, did Joe have a brother or sister living somewhere?

A feeling of emptiness filled his heart. A dark cloud covered his senses. His throat tightened, his hands began to tremble, and small beads of sweat appeared on his brow. The images of the dream had reoccurred, he couldn't move, the spider came closer and closer. He felt an evil force attached to the images and the force penetrated his very soul. He shook his head and forced the visions and thoughts out of his mind; nothing was going to interfere with the pleasure he was going to have with Louise today. A single stab of pain flickered behind his left eye. The visions remained in the subconscious realm of his mind.

Joe wheeled his car into a parking space at the Oasis Liquor Store. The parking lot, which had been completely filled a half hour earlier, was now almost empty. A small bell attached to the door announced his entrance into the store. He scanned the rows of shelves containing an array of different-shaped bottles. He selected a bottle of Jamaican rum and a fifth of Jack Daniels.

From the coolers in the back of the store he took six-packs of Coke and 7-Up and a five-pound sack of ice cubes. "That should loosen her up," he thought. He paid for the items at the counter and as he left the little bell on the door tingled again. "Guess I'm all set," he said to himself as he placed the ice and pop in a portable cooler in the trunk of his car.

Joe turned off the paved street onto the abandoned road leading to the log cabin where Louise had agreed to meet him. The road was overgrown with weeds. Small saplings had sprung up in the ruts and past rains had washed a small gully diagonally across his path. "Damn," Joe said aloud, "I hope I don't get hung up back here." He saw the cabin in a grove of trees hiding it from the main road. His heart quickened when he saw her standing in the doorway, her long legs clad in a pair of skin-tight Levis.

The car bounced to a sudden stop in front of the cabin. "Hi," she said, making a small waving gesture with her hand. "I didn't know if you were going to make it down that old road or not."

The first time he had seen her she had her hair braided in long pigtails. Today it hung softly in long golden curls, accentuating her high cheekbones and making her appear older than her nineteen years.

Joe eagerly took her into his arms and crushed her lips with a passionate kiss. She started to respond, then pulled away. "Let's go for a walk down by the creek " she said, pointing behind the cabin. Pulling him by the arm, she darted through the heavy underbrush, ducking to miss the low-hanging branches of the trees. She suddenly stopped. They had come to a clearing in the trees. Directly in front of her, almost hidden by the lush, green grass on its banks, was a small stream with swift-moving water. "Isn't it beautiful and pleasant here, so quiet and nobody around," she said. "I spend a lot of time here by myself. Last week I found the spring up the hill there where this creek comes from. The water is so cold and so fresh. Try it," she said, as she knelt and scooped a handful to her mouth.

Joe sat down in the soft grass beside her. Grasping her shoulders, he gently pulled her back from the edge of the creek. She laid back in the grass with her arms above her head. She moaned softly as Joe found her breast. There was little foreplay. Their bodies locked together in pleasure. Their passions exploded quickly.

On their way back to the log cabin, she asked him, "Do you love me?"

"Sure do," he said. "I could make love to you all day long." Back at the car, he opened the trunk, took out the cooler, and mixed them each a drink. Handing her the rum and Coke drink he had mixed, he said, "Sweetheart, you're terrific." She responded with parted lips exposing the tip of her tongue. Joe felt desire building in his groin again.

A few miles down the road, Moe winced at the pinging sound from the engine of the patrol car as he turned off the ignition. He knew that a tune-up was overdue. He had delayed asking the city for money to service it since their budget was almost depleted for the year. After leaving Mary, he had made two patrol runs down highway 65. The traffic had thinned down and everything seemed back to normal.

There had been a time when he would have welcomed some unusual activity: apprehending a drunk driver, chasing a speeding vehicle, making a U-turn on a two-lane highway at fifty-five miles per hour with the blare of his siren in his ears. He didn't need that type of excitement anymore; he was the happiest when he could help a motorist change a flat tire or furnish them a gallon of gas to make it to the next station. He got a great deal of contentment out of offering a runaway teenager his home as a place to spend the night, talking to them about their troubles.

His wife was thumbing through an old magazine as he entered his office. She looked up and pressed a finger to her lips, pointing to the cot where Moe Jr. lay sleeping. "Any calls while I was out?"

"No, it's been real boring, and the noise of that fan could drive someone loony."

The young boy on the cot stirred, opened his eyes and smiled when he saw his father. "Can I hear the siren now?" he asked.

Moe looked at his wife and said, "I think I'll have the switchboard operator ring me at home if any calls come to the office phone. That way I can spend part of the afternoon with you and Moe Jr."

The siren of the patrol car pierced the air as they drove up Main Street to their small two-bedroom bungalow.

Seven

The grandstand was almost filled by the time Al and Roy Lee found their seats. They were sitting directly above the entrance to the arena with the animal chutes on either side. Perfect spot, thought Al; they would have a direct view of all the activities. There was excitement in the air.

The high school marching band from Carville was performing precision marching routines. The music was intoxicating to the crowd. People began to clap in rhythm and stamp their feet. A cheer went up when six pretty young girls, clad in sparkling gold halters and shorts, twirled batons in unison. The band stopped playing and the baton twirlers froze in position with their batons crossing their chests. A prancing, majestic, bleached palomino stallion entered the arena. The rider was dressed in a white rhinestone cowboy shirt and black pants. Flying high above his head was an American flag on a pole fixed in the saddle and held firmly by the rider. Slightly behind on both sides were riders on black steeds, one carrying the state flag and the other the rodeo banner, which depicted a red bucking bronco on a white background. A lone trumpet from somewhere in the band announced their entrance. Quiet filled the grandstand to a point where one could have heard a pin drop. The band struck up "The Star-Spangled Banner." The crowd rose in unison and most people placed their right hand over their heart.

The announcer came over the loudspeaker, "Welcome, ladies and gentlemen, to the sixth annual Carville Rodeo! And here to open the activities is our very own Edward Welsh, chairman of the rodeo committee."

"Thank you, thank you," the nasal twang echoed in the loudspeaker. "I want to thank all you good people out there that have helped me make this occasion possible. It's taken a lot of hard work, but I think we have put together a very fine program that the city of Carville can be proud of."

The performance formally started with a grand parade. There was row after row of cowboys and cowgirls on well-groomed horses wearing gold- and silver-studded saddles. A team of mules driven by a clown pulled a two-wheeled cart with square wheels. Cowboys did magic, twirling long loops of rope. A stagecoach carried the queen of the rodeo, who leaned out the window throwing kisses to the crowd. Clowns being chased by a billy goat rolled and tumbled in the dirt.

Roy Lee was intrigued by all the pageantry and glamour. He wondered if he could ever be a cowboy and join the rodeo. After the parade had exited the arena there was a synchronized performance by sixteen riders on matching sorrel Quarter horses. They moved en masse as if they were a single body.

"Dad, how much would a horse like that cost?" Roy Lee asked.

"Too much, plus there's a lot of work taking care of them," Al replied. "You have to brush them down every day, comb their tail and mane, trim their hooves, and exercise them a lot."

"If I had one I'd take good care of him," Roy Lee said.

They watched the calf-roping competition. Roy Lee felt sorry for the young calves, the way their heads were twisted around by the choking ropes. He watched the bucking broncos come out of the chutes directly below him, their backs arched high and their legs stiff with twisting bodies. He stood up and cheered with the crowd when the rider was able to stay mounted until the bell rang. Al shared the excitement with his son. He knew what fantasies were going through Roy Lee's mind. He had the same fantasies as a young man years ago at his first rodeo. The dreams were so vivid, the thundering hooves under him and the sound of the rope twirling around his head as he prepared to rope a calf. Al bought a large sack of buttered popcorn and two glasses of lemonade.

Time passed quickly. The bulldogging event and the saddle bronc riding competition were soon over. The last competition of the day was the Brahma bull riding. Roy Lee sat on the edge of his seat as the first contestant was announced over the loudspeaker: "And now out of chute #3, contestant #29, riding Black Thunder."

The gate swung open, and a low bellow emanated from the huge beast as it exploded out of the chute. The bull's body seemed to be suspended in air, a quivering mass of muscle. The rider, only allowed to hold onto the rope around the bull with one hand, held the other hand high above his head to help maintain balance. The eight-second bell rang, indicating the rider had stayed on the bull the minimum required time. The rider dismounted by sliding off the side of the bull. When he hit the ground the animal wheeled with fury. Lowering its head, the bull prepared to charge. Two arena clowns ran toward the bull, making loud noises and waving red bandannas. The confused bull began pawing the ground and making short snorting sounds. This gave the cowboy the split second that he needed. He leaped to his feet and ran to the wooden fence enclosing the arena. The bull's horns missed him by only a few inches as he went over the top board of the fence. The judges gave the cowboy a score of 82 for his efforts. Three more contestants tried their luck at bullriding. Only one stayed astride his animal for the required eight seconds. The judges gave him a score of 79.

There was a commotion below them. A large brown bull was violently trying to bust out of the gate of chute #1. The loudspeaker came alive. "Now out of chute #1, contestant #32, riding the granddaddy of Brahma bulls, Old Sugar Foot." The adrenaline welled up in Roy Lee's bloodstream. This was Tex, the cowboy friend he had made earlier in the day. He said a prayer for Tex, praying that he wouldn't get hurt by the bull. The crowd roared as the animal shot forth from the chute. It turned a full 180 degrees in the air, hitting the ground so hard it fell on its back haunches. Then, regaining its posture, it leaped into the air shaking its head, its body twisting in a demonic rage.

Roy Lee held his breath and counted silently to eight. "Why doesn't the bell go off?" he thought.

When the bell rang, the rider slid off the bull and hit the ground running for the fence. Freed from the annoyance on its back, the bull stood still in the middle of the arena. With hatred in its beady eyes it focused on one of the arena clowns that was trying to coax it to the exit gate. With a burst of speed it charged. The clown had misjudged the distance between him and the bull and the speed of the charge. The bull caught the clown in the middle of his back as the clown had turned to run. With a mighty upward movement of its head, the bull sent the clown flying into the air. The body lay motionless as it hit the ground. Two other clowns immediately approached the bull to distract him from their colleague. Old Sugar Foot was finally lured out the exit gate. They carried the injured clown off on a stretcher. The judges gave Tex a score of 93. No other contestant came close to beating him. Roy Lee was happy for his friend.

The sixteen-year-old Tad sat alone in the non-reserved seating area of the bleachers at the east end of the arena. He had saved a seat beside him, hoping his father would join him for the performance. The boy's physical traits resembled his father's. He was well-built with handsome facial features. He was a very sensitive young man. His demure character stemmed from his mother's personality. His childhood had been traumatic. His tyrannical grandfather dominated his every action, which repressed any development of self-worth and increased his shyness. Early on, he had found solitude an effective avenue of escape from the demands of his grandfather. He would retreat to his room or a secluded spot in the grove of trees behind their house, with his little palette of paints. He painted crude pictures of smiling animals. Occasionally he would sketch human figures, but they always had expressions of sorrow on their faces.

If asked to express his feelings for his mother, Tad could have only answered, "pity." He sensed an inner creativeness in her which lay barren because she was too timid to express it. The only time it had ever come to the surface was when he was a young child and she had read Elizabethan sonnets to him at bedtime. He could still remember her expressive interpretations as she read the rhythmic lines of poetry. Tad was confused as to his relationship with his father. Was he really a father? He didn't live with them, and he was married to someone other than his mother. He knew he displeased his father at times. On his fourteenth birthday his father had gotten him a single-shot .410 shotgun. They had gone rabbit hunting the next weekend. His father had shot the first rabbit that came scurrying out of the brier patch. When they walked up to it, Tad looked at the mangled body with its torn fur speckled with blood. He dropped his shotgun and turned and vomited in the snow.

On another occasion, the first time Joe had taken him fishing, he had become upset when Joe tried to show him how to put a worm on a hook. When he had refused to try, Joe had called him a sissy. He knew that he could never explain to his father that he wasn't afraid of doing it, it was just that he didn't want to cause pain to any living creature.

As the events of the rodeo were coming to an end, Rosie

labored in the kitchen preparing the evening meal. She lifted the lid on the roaster. Steam escaped from the hot pork roast sizzling from the drippings in the bottom of the pan. She was preparing Joe's favorite meal. Later she would put potatoes and carrots in with the roast and when everything had finished cooking, she'd make brown gravy from the drippings.

She had spent all day planning for the evening after Joe got home from the rodeo. She had put her hair up in curlers. Sorting through her closet she had finally found a sheath dress that she could still squeeze into. It was black and cut low in the front. Joe had liked the dress when she first got because it revealed the ample cleavage of her breasts. She wondered if he would notice them this evening. To complement the candle-light meal she had planned, she purchased a bottle of red wine. On the spur of the moment, she had picked up a bottle of B&B for after-dinner drinks. Satisfied that the roast would be done on time, she replaced the lid on the roaster. Taking off her apron, she walked into the bedroom. She had placed the record player on the stand next to the bed. Joe had always enjoyed listening to country and western music while they were making love. She sorted through the records in the music rack, picking out Joe's favorites. A glow of anticipation warmed her body. It had been a long time since she had looked forward to having sex. It had become a mechanical ritual between Joe and her. Tonight would be different; she felt ten years younger. She would tease Joe like she used to, refusing his advances at first, then when his passions began to boil she would make violent love to him. When she walked out of the bedroom she looked at her body, reflected in the full-length mirror in the hallway. What she saw in her mind was the figure she had at age twenty-five. If only Joe could remember her the same way.

Meanwhile, Joe picked up the half-empty bottle of Jack Daniels and poured himself another drink. He looked at Louise lying next to him on a blanket. She was completely nude, her hair matted with sweat. There were small red bruises on her neck. Her eyes were closed and there was a faint smile of contentment on her face. He couldn't remember how many times they had made love. She opened her eyes and looked up at him. "Want to do it again?" she asked. He looked at his watch and was startled to see how late it was. "I've got to pick up my son at the rodeo, I'm already late," he said. Quickly he dressed, not taking time to button his shirt, and headed toward his car.

She was still nude when he drove off. "Call me sometime," she yelled, as he gunned the car down the abandoned road. She watched the car and was surprised that he made it to the highway the way he was driving. With squealing tires, he turned north on highway 65.

"And now, ladies and gentlemen, let's give all our contestants a round of applause," crackled the loudspeaker, "and thank you all for coming; remember, we have four more performances, so if you liked what you saw today, come back. We recommend that you visit the midway before you leave this afternoon, and if you're hungry try some of the food at one of the concession stands sponsored by our local churches. You'll be supporting a good cause. Drive careful when you get out on the highway."

Roy Lee stood on the seat next to Al and clapped loudly. Most of the contestants had entered the arena. Turning to face the grandstand, they waved their ten-gallon hats in appreciation of the standing ovation the crowd had given them. Roy Lee spotted his cowboy friend. "There's Tex," he said to Al. "I'm going to congratulate him." Bounding down the steps to the first row of seats, he leaned over the rail, waving his hands. He caught the young cowboy's eye. "Good ride on Old Sugar Foot. He sure was a mean one."

"Thanks," said the cowboy, "this is the first time I have ever taken first place. I plan to come back next year. Maybe I'll run into you then."

It was crowded getting through the midway to the parking lot. Most of the entrances to the sideshows had long lines of people waiting to get in. They went by the burlesque tent; the pretty lady was still taking tickets. Very few cars were leaving the parking lot as Al drove between long, even rows of parked cars toward the exit gate. "You're ready to go home, aren't you?" Al asked.

"Yes, I want to get home and tell Mom about all about the rodeo."

They drove around the outskirts of Carville, then turned south on highway 65. Roy Lee leaned his head back in the seat; a shroud of drowsiness engulfed him. Al looked over at his son sitting in the seat next to him. His eyes were closed. The excitement must have worn him out, Al thought.

Eight

Mary took the apple pie out of the oven and set it on the kitchen table to cool. Gene, sitting at the table coloring pictures in an old newspaper, savored the aroma. "A-a-are y-you going to f-fix whipped c-c-cream to put on it?" he asked.

"Sure, I'll even put some cinnamon in it. You sure are doing a good job coloring," she said, looking at the newspaper spread out on the table. "You should save that and show it to your dad when he gets home."

What a difference between the two oldest children, she thought. Roy Lee looked more like his father every day. Even though he was slight of build, his small body had a sinewy appearance. His face was lean, with high cheekbones and a square chin. Gene had his mother's features, an oval face with dimples in his cheeks. He was short like his mother and tended to be rather roly-poly.

Gene had been born with feet that turned inward at the toes, and he had trouble learning to walk. Mary had spent hours holding his feet outward in a normal position. The doctor had assured her that he would outgrow the deformity. Then when he started talking he had trouble saying certain words, which developed into a stammering process. It pained Mary to see the troubled look on his face when he was unable to form the sounds to make a word. The doctor wasn't as optimistic about him outgrowing the stammering problem.

The clock on the kitchen wall chimed the hour of four. They should be home before too long, she thought. I should start peeling the potatoes and get the chicken frying.

On the kitchen table was a box wrapped in tissue paper and decorated with a homemade ribbon. It was a present for Roy Lee. Even though his birthday had been six months earlier, she had decided to get him a special present to celebrate the day. She had purchased a pair of work pants for him to wear to school the coming year. He was one of the last ones in his school to wear bib overalls to class. She knew he had withstood a lot of teasing because he "dressed like a farmer." Not once had he complained, knowing that they were too poor to buy "city clothes."

Roy Lee had been asleep ever since they had left Carville. The traffic was very light; only one car had passed them. Al yawned deeply, wishing he could take a short nap. The turn-off to the farm was just a half mile further, so it wouldn't be long before he could relax in his overstuffed chair. He eased back on the accelerator as he approached the country lane which led to the farmhouse. The car shuddered as its wheels left the smooth face of the cement and made contact with the ruts in the dirt road. Al brought the car to a stop, planning to get the mail out of the rural delivery box. The sudden change in motion awoke Roy Lee.

"Let me get the mail," Roy Lee said.

"All right" his father agreed, "but watch out for cars." The mailbox was attached to a post on the other side of the highway.

* * *

About a mile south on the highway, Joe squinted at the dials on his wristwatch. He had trouble bringing them into focus. "Four-thirty," he said aloud. "I hope Tad doesn't call Rosie to see why I'm late." An oncoming car blared its horn as Joe weaved over the center line. "Asshole," Joe said. He peered down at the speedometer. "Did it really read 80 miles per hour? He never saw the boy on the highway. He faintly remembered the sound of the impact and seeing something fly over the hood. With his brain numbed with alcohol it did not occur to him to stop.

Al noticed the speeding vehicle out of the corner of his eye. He glanced quickly in the rear view mirror. He saw the body flung into the air a split second after he heard the sickening thud of metal striking flesh. Time seemed to stop; the body was suspended in space. A scream escaped Al's lips. He opened the car door and bolted the forty yards down the highway where the body had been thrown. Horror filled his heart as he saw the crumpled extremities, the blood, and the battered face.

Mabel had been sitting on her back porch when she noticed Al turn on to the dirt road and stop. She had heard the squeal of tires and saw Al dash across the highway and out of sight down the road. She stood up, peering over the corn stalks that blocked her view, but was unable see what was happening. Walking out her driveway, she came to the side of the highway. She could see Al kneeling by the side of the road. Suddenly she realized what had happened. She turned toward the house and screamed, "Karl, Karl!" Her oldest son appeared in the doorway. "*Kommen sie schnell*!" she screamed. "Take Herr Al to der hospital."

Al gently gathered Roy Lee into his arms. He knew there was nothing that could be done to prevent the ebbing of life from the small broken body. He held him close and his large teardrops mixed with the streaks of blood on Roy Lee's bib overalls. The lifeless body hung limp in his arms.

Karl screeched to a stop beside the kneeling figure with the boy in his arms. Al got in the passenger side and instantly Karl stepped on the accelerator. Time seemed to stop. Al's mind became a void. The world around him was suspended in a state of nothingness. There was no sound, no visual image, no sensation of the body in his arms. A state of shock protected him from reality.

"I'll go get Mary," said Karl, as he opened the car door for Al. They were parked near the entrance to the emergency room at the back of the hospital. Al's mind snapped back to the present and with it came the horror of what had happened. He looked down at the boy in his arms and wondered how much pain his heart could stand. No sooner had he entered the hospital than the intercom announced a "code blue." Two nurses met him in the hallway with a gurney.

They took the still body from his arms. Another nurse took Al tenderly by the hand and led him to the waiting room. She guided him to an austere wooden chair and without asking if he cared for any, poured him a cup of strong black coffee.

Al sat on the edge of the chair, staring into space. His brain was numbed with disbelief. Sorrow filled his heart. How could life be so fragile, especially in someone so young who hadn't really experienced the pleasures of living yet? The question "Why?" burned in his mind, searing his soul. No answers came.

Mary was relieved to see the car coming down the dirt road. She had become concerned at the lateness of the hour, wondering why Al and Roy Lee weren't home from the rodeo. Amazement, then apprehension, rose within her when she saw Karl and Mabel in the front seat of the car. She ran out the front door and in a voice nearing the edge of hysteria cried, "Where's Al and Roy Lee?"

With his arm around her waist, Karl helped his sobbing mother up the front porch steps. "There's been an accident," he said as they met Mary on the landing. "I'll take you to the hospital. Mom will stay with your kids."

"Are they both hurt?" Mary asked as Karl turned the car around in the driveway.

"Just Roy Lee."

"How bad?" Karl couldn't answer. He just stared straight ahead and shook his head slowly from side to side.

The foreboding thoughts she had experienced earlier in the day returned. Her heart whispered to her in anguish, telling her that Roy Lee was gone. There were no tears; she couldn't cry. As she walked into the emergency room, Mary saw Dr. Kern standing beside Al with his hand on his shoulder. He was talking to Al in a hushed voice. "Hello, Mary," Dr. Kern sadly greeted her. "I'm sorry, but there was nothing I could do to save him. The only consolation I can give you is that he died instantly. He did not have to suffer."

Anger tore at Mary's heart. What about her suffering? Was the plague of suffering a reward for the living? She confronted God. It isn't fair, you tested me once. You took my precious daughter from me. What have I done to deserve yet another child to be taken from me? If you are a just and loving God, restore the life of my son! The tears came. Mary fell to the floor, her body convulsing on the cold linoleum vinyl.

Al tenderly picked Mary up in his arms and buried his head in her hair. "I'm sorry," Al said as he choked back his sobs. "I shouldn't have let him cross the road to get the mail. Why? Why didn't I think? I've lost the most precious thing of my life. A part of me has been torn away. Life can never be the same without him. He was such a little character, so good-hearted and lovable. How can I ever live with myself knowing I was responsible?"

The trembling of Mary's body slowly subsided as Al gently rocked her in his arms. Slowly she opened her eyes and saw the pain on Al's face. She pulled him close and said, "We must go on living; we still have Gene and Jimmy."

The traffic was getting heavy as Moe parked the patrol car on an overpass on highway 65. He watched as a car pulled out of the line of traffic and barely squeezed back into the lane in time to miss an oncoming car. "Crazy fool," Moe thought. "Where do some people learn to drive? No use pulling the guy over, it would just tie up traffic more." He looked at his watch. "In about an hour the traffic should start thinning down," he mused. Then he could get home and have supper with his wife and son. He dozed briefly, basking in the rays of the setting sun that filtered through the tinted windshield of the patrol car. He was startled when the radio broke the silence.

That had to be his wife. Pressing the transmission button he answered, "Yes, honey, what's up?"

"The hospital called, there's been an accident. Some one died. They didn't give me any names or the circumstances."

"I'm on my way now," he said, as the patrol car came alive. The tires squealed as he made a sharp U-turn and the eerie scream of the siren ripped through the air.

Moe entered the emergency door of the hospital. Fear gripped his body when he saw Mary in the hallway on a cot with an IV attached to her arm. Dr. Kern saw him come in and quickly explained to him that Mary had gone into shock learning that Roy Lee had died.

Moe shoved his emotions aside and became the professional he was trained to be. "What happened?" he asked.

"I don't really know; Al brought Roy Lee in about forty minutes ago. He said a car had hit him north of town near the road to their farm. There was nothing I could do to save him. I swear every bone in his body was broken. I'm sorry I didn't contact you sooner but in all the excitement it slipped my mind."

"Where's Al now?" Moe asked.

"He's sitting in my office. I think he's coherent enough to fill you in on what happened. Feel free to use my office to talk to him."

The short distance from the emergency room to Dr. Kern's office took what seemed like a lifetime to travel. All the fond memories he had of Al during their long relationship passed through his mind. He opened the door to the office. Al sat, slumped over and dejected, in an overstuffed leather chair.

"I'm so sorry, Al," Moe began. "I wish I could ease the pain you must have. Can you tell me what happened?"

Al recounted the events surrounding the accident as best he could.

"What kind of a car was it? What color? Did you see who was driving it?" Moe ran through the questions rapidly.

Al buried his head in the palms of his hands. Everything was a blur. It had happened so quickly. It seemed so long ago.

"Was the car speeding?" Moe continued.

"I think so, he was going pretty fast. He could have been doing close to eighty miles an hour."

Moe looked up from the spiral notebook he was scribbling on. "You said 'he,' was it a man driving?"

"I don't know."

"Were there any other cars that went by right before or after the accident?"

"I don't remember any. The only thing I can remember is when I picked Roy Lee up, Karl was beside the road in my car."

Back at his office, Moe had put out an APB to all the law enforcement units in the surrounding counties, asking if anyone had seen a speeding vehicle any time late in the afternoon.

"Not much to go on," thought Moe as he turned north on highway 65 and headed for the scene of the accident. "Maybe Al will remember some details after he gets over the shock."

Moe spotted the dark stain of dried blood on the edge of the cement about forty yards north of Al's mailbox. As he got out of the patrol car, he made a mental note that there were no skid marks any place on the highway. Whoever had hit Roy Lee hadn't even attempted to stop. He searched the side of the road very carefully, hoping to find something that would give him a clue to identify the car or person that had been involved in the accident. He picked up a square piece of blood-stained paper. It was a picture of a cowboy on a bucking Brahma bull. He turned it over and saw the words, "To my friend Roy Lee from Tex Oakes," inscribed on the back. Putting it in a plastic bag, he laid it on the front seat of the patrol car.

Moe searched the sides of the road a quarter of a mile both north and south of the spot where the dried blood was on the highway. The only thing he found was one of Roy Lee's work shoes. Even though it was still tightly laced, it had been torn from his foot. He went over the facts that he had scribbled in his dog-eared spiral notebook: time—4:30 to 4:40 p.m.—vehicle going north on highway 65 at a high rate of speed—heading toward Carville—probably hadn't been to the rodeo—very little traffic on highway at the time—no skid marks—driver hadn't attempted to stop—victim thrown forty to fifty yards after impact—could have been dragged part of the distance but observer saw body fly in air—doctor reported severe total body trauma.

He knew that each bit of information he had was important, like a piece to a puzzle. Each piece was important if you could find the right place to put it. All the pieces didn't have to be present. If you just had enough to give a general idea of the picture, you knew what you were looking for to fill in the missing spaces.

Three messages had come in over his office telephone line for him to call when he got home. "I've been holding supper for you," his wife said. "Can you eat now?"

"You and Moe Jr. go ahead and eat. I want to check out these phone calls to see if they have anything to do with an accident that happened out north of town this afternoon."

"Yes, I heard a young boy died. He was the son of your friend Al, wasn't he? It's so sad, especially when it's someone you know."

He dialed the phone numbers his wife had written down. All three were concerned with the APB he had put out. They involved reports of arrests made of individuals driving under the influence of alcohol. The time and location of the arrests made it impossible for any of the individuals to have anything to do with the accident.

Moe knew that the more time that went by without any concrete information the greater the chance that the accident might go unsolved. He decided to contact the local radio stations and ask them to put out a public plea for information anyone might have concerning the accident.

Moe Hendersen took a pragmatic approach to his work, noting even the smallest details in his investigations. A slow and mechanical thoroughness gave him the confidence that any case could be solved. However, this evening a feeling of desperation crept into his thoughts. He had to solve this case. His best friend's child had been killed by what was apparently a hit-and-run driver. Also, for Mary's sake, he had to find out what happened.

Nine

His sweat-covered palms tightly gripped the steering wheel as he tried to focus on the road ahead of him. There was a steady line of cars in the oncoming lane. Joe shook his head, trying to clear the web of shadows from his brain. The alcohol-induced numbness of his muscles required him to consciously direct his body to make movements that otherwise would have been automatic reflexes. Fragmented thoughts kept creeping into his mind, "I hit something—on the road—what was it—an animal—could it have been a person?"

A service station appeared on the right-hand side of the highway. His tires squealed as he almost missed the turn-off. Parking at the rear of the station, he fumbled for the car door handle. After several attempts he opened the door, and steadying himself with his hand on the car fender, made his way to the front of the car.

At first Joe didn't notice any damage. Then, on closer inspection, he saw the broken grille. At first he thought the front of the hood was covered with bug spots, then he shivered when he realized that it was blood. An object was wedged under the bumper of the car. He reached down, pulling on it until it came loose. His stomach tightened as he looked at the small work shoe in his hand. It seemed to burn his hand. Dropping it, he kicked it under a trash receptacle near the back door of the gas station.

Joe's mind began to clear as the adrenaline surged through his body. "I have to think what to do. I've got to get rid of any evidence that might link me to an accident."

He slipped on his sunglasses and pulled his hat down over his forehead. As he walked around to the front of the service station, the attendent was busy servicing three cars at the gas pumps. Joe quickly scanned the occupants of the three cars. Thank goodness, he thought, I don't recognize anyone.

"Howdy," Joe said as he approached the attendent. "Could I get a bucket of water to wash off the front end of my car? I hit a pheasant down the road and I want to wash the blood off before it dries."

"Sure, help yourself," replied the attendent. "I'd do it for you, but I'm busy as heck here. Must be the rodeo traffic."

Joe filled the bucket with water four times, splashing it on the front of his car and rubbing away the specks of blood.

Satisfied that he had removed all of the blood, Joe pulled back onto highway 65 and headed toward the entrance gate to the rodeo. He knew he was late. He wondered where Tad would be. He hoped that he hadn't called Rosie.

Tad had been waiting by the entrance gate for over twenty minutes. Had his father forgotten about him? Could he have been in an accident? Tad spotted his father in the far lane of traffic about half a block away. He threaded his way through the traffic to get to the other side of the road. "Hi" he said as he got into the car. "You sure missed an exciting rodeo. What did you do, get tied up with a client?"

"Yes, it took me longer than I thought."

Tad noted a distraught tone in his father's voice. The air inside the car reeked of alcohol. It bothered him that his father drank so much. Knowing how surly his father could get when he was in this type of mood, Tad remained silent until they reached his grandfather's house.

"Thanks for letting me go to the rodeo," Tad said as he walked around the front of the car. "Do you know you have a broken grille?"

"Yes, I hit a deer on the highway the other day."

Funny, thought Tad, I didn't notice it when he picked me up this morning.

Rosie paced the kitchen floor. Joe should have been home by now. Picking up the phone, she dialed Tad's number. She quickly replaced the receiver before the first ring was completed. She knew that the old man, Tad's grandfather, would probably answer and she would have to listen to his tirade about what a worthless human being her husband was. Ever since his daughter's divorce the old man had been possessed with animosity toward Joe. He let the whole community know that Joe had abandoned his wife and child to marry a whore.

The black sheath dress she had on was becoming uncomfortable. She had managed to hold in her stomach when she first put it on, but now her waist bulged tightly against the sheer material. The seams on the side were precariously close to coming apart. There were sweat stains on the front next to her cleavage.

The squeal of the rusty hinges on the garage door brought a sigh of relief from Rosie. Fluffing her freshly curled hair with the opened fingers of her hand, she checked her make-up in the hallway mirror. With a small crumpled tissue she removed some misplaced mascara from the corner of her eye.

"Hello, honey," she said, greeting Joe with open arms as he came in the back door from the garage. As she came close to him she smelled the alcohol on his breath. There was a strange look on his face. His eyes were perplexed with a glint of fear. He appeared old and depressed. She knew the effect that alcohol had on him. It could totally change his personality. One minute he would seem normal and then suddenly he would go into a rage, ranting and raving as if demons were torturing his thoughts. Madness would seem to claim his mind. The look in his eyes was different, though, today. It was as if he was on the verge of panic. Rosie had learned not to confront Joe about his drinking when he was in one of these mental states. It only made him worse, and once he had physically abused her when she had suggested that maybe he drank too much. The best thing to do was to act as if nothing was wrong and in time he would return to his old self.

"Don't smear your damn lipstick all over my face," he snarled as Rosie attempted to kiss him on the cheek.

"Sorry. Did you have fun at the rodeo?"

"Didn't go, got all tied up with a client," he snapped, indicating he didn't want to talk about it.

"I have a surprise for you. I fixed your favorite meal."

"I'm not hungry."

"Aw, please, Joe, eat something. I worked all afternoon preparing a meal for you, hoping to make you happy and let you know how much I love you."

Joe begrudgingly took his place at the small kitchen table. Rosie decided to forego the wine since she didn't want to enhance Joe's foul mood with any additional alcohol. She piled their plates high with steaming chunks of roast beef, carrots and potatoes and topped them with brown gravy.

They ate in silence. Rosie attacked her food with a fork in one hand and a hard crust roll in the other. She savored the taste of the rich gravy, soaking it up with the roll and biting through the hard crust with the teeth in the corner of her mouth. Joe ate sparingly, moving his food around on his plate. The taste of the food did not register in his mind.

"Why don't you go in and take a nap on the sofa while I clean up the dishes," Rosie said. "I'll find some good country music on the radio for you." Rosie finished wiping the dishes and took off her apron. She noted a spot of gravy on the front of her sheath dress. She tried removing it with a damp cloth, but a stain remained. Things were not going the way she had planned. She had been excited all afternoon thinking about how she would aggressively seduce Joe when he got home. Her excitement began to dwindle. She hesitated, then decided that maybe some B&B would change his mood. She poured out a generous shot of the thick liquid in each of two brandy glasses. Joe was staring off into space as she entered the living room. "How about some B&B to get relaxed?"

"No," answered Joe. "I've got a headache. I'm going to bed." He didn't notice the tears that welled up in her eyes as he went into the bedroom.

Rosie drank the first B&B in one gulp and chased it with the second. Sitting on the edge of the sofa, she silently sobbed. What had she done wrong? When she was younger, she could lure any man into bed. She enjoyed the teasing, the foreplay and then the repeated sexual orgasms. She still had fantasies and needs, but men didn't look at her anymore with desire and passion in their eyes. Had she become repulsive to the opposite sex? She coughed as she chain-lit her fourth cigarette.

Joe lay awake in his bed. Snores drifted in from the living room where Rosie had fallen asleep on the sofa. Torturing questions kept echoing in his mind. Did he kill someone? Could he have saved a life if he had stopped? Would he go to jail? Would Rosie find out about Louise?

The pain started somewhere behind his left eye. Like an eddy, it vibrated outwards until it encompassed his whole head. He could feel the blood pounding through the blood vessels in his brain. Nausea gripped his stomach. The pain was so intense that for a few fleeting seconds he would have welcomed death. Joe fumbled for the brown bottle sitting on the bottom shelf of the medicine cabinet. Dr. Macke had prescribed a strong narcotic for him to take when the pain occurred. There were two capsules left in the bottle. Joe put both of them in his mouth. He drank sparingly from a plastic glass, just enough to swallow the capsules. Joe lay motionless in bed. Any movement would intensify the pain. The numbing action of the narcotic began to invade his brain. Slowly the pain decreased. He could almost picture pain as an object floating out of his body into space. As the penetration of a deep sleep eased his tormented state, his conscious mind decreased in activity. His subconscious mind began to stir.

The black spider descended from its web, coming closer and closer to Joe. He could feel the heat of its breath on his face. It was evil. Its multifaceted eyes reflected sinister rays of power. Joe could hear himself screaming, but he couldn't move. He was paralyzed. The spider came closer and closer. The hairy legs touched his body. The very fires of hell burned his chest. Venom erupted from its proboscis. Joe bolted upright in bed, gasping for breath. The sheet covering his body was soaked in sweat. He shook his head violently. The vision didn't want to leave his conscious thought. He fought for control of his mind.

A sound startled Joe. It was Rosie still snoring on the sofa. The clock on the table beside the bed read 4:15 A.M. That was the worst the nightmare had ever been. He needed something to calm his nerves. The early morning rays of sunlight had begun to filter over the horizon, filling the house with an eerie glow. The B&B was sitting on the kitchen counter. He poured a double shot into a plastic glass. Sitting at the kitchen table, he slowly sipped the dark rich liquid. It sent a warm glow through his body. A tiredness overcame him, but he was afraid to go back to bed. Afraid that the spider would return. With his elbows on the table and his chin resting in the palms of his hands, he dozed. He reached the stage of semisleep without the nightmare returning.

He awoke as Rosie was fixing coffee in the percolator. "How long you been sitting there?" she asked.

"Not long. The coffee sure smells good. Why did you sleep on the sofa last night?"

"Well, you went to bed early and I just fell asleep reading."

He looked at her eyes, still streaked with tears. The curls had disappeared overnight and her hair laid flat against her head. Even though she had gained weight and time had not been particularly kind to her face, there was still something that was attractive to him. "I'm sorry," he said. "I was tired and didn't feel good last night. I did appreciate the supper you fixed for me."

A gleam of hope filled her eyes. Rosie was surprised when Joe tuned in a news station on the radio as they sat down for breakfast. Usually the only thing he would listen to was country music. "When did you become so interested in the news?" she asked.

"I thought it would be nice to know what's going on in the world."

Joe had just finished breakfast and poured a second cup of coffee when the announcement came over the radio. "...and now for the local news. A nine-year-old rural Laynard boy was killed on highway 65 north at approximately 4:20 P.M. yesterday. Authorities are calling it a hit-and-run accident. Anyone with any information concerning the accident is asked to contact Moe Hendersen, chief of police, at the city hall in Laynard."

Joe stiffened in his chair. Panic engulfed him. Had he killed a nine-year-old child? The coffee cup slipped from his hand and banged on the table, spewing hot coffee into the air. He felt trapped; the kitchen walls were closing in on him.

"I've got to be in the office early today," he said, standing up abruptly. He was gone before Rosie could speak. She pondered his strange actions as she cleaned up the coffee on the table top.

The pillage of guilt touched his moral fibers. Joe knew that he should turn himself in. It had been an accident. He hadn't done it on purpose. What if it was found out that he had been drinking? What if they asked him why he hadn't stopped? What if his escapade with Louise became known?

As he drove down the road, a deep and emotional turmoil tugged at his mind. Conflicting mental debates on right and wrong traumatized his rationality. His conscious mind came to a conclusion. Why should he turn himself in? It was an accident. It could have happened to anyone. He wasn't a criminal. The boy was dead, nothing could bring him back.

Why should anyone else have to suffer? A feeling of relief came over Joe. He knew he had made the right decision. If anyone had recognized him or could identify his car they would have arrested him by now and the chief of police wouldn't be asking the public for information. He also trusted that Louise would not disclose their lovemaking at the abandoned log cabin. Satisfied that silence was his best action, he mentally removed the incident from his conscious mind. It quietly slipped into his subconscious.

Early that morning, Moe made a special trip to the county courthouse in Carville to pick up the coroner's report. Back in his patrol car, he unsealed the envelope and removed the official-looking document. The report was quite short: "Approximately nine-year-old Caucasian male. Cause of death: multiple trauma, consistent with police report that victim had been hit by a car. The body was fully clothed except for shoes." He started to fold the sheet of paper, then looked again at the last line. He reread the word shoes. Was this a typing error? Were both shoes missing or only one? Moe recalled that he had only found one shoe at the site of the accident even though he had made a thorough search of the area. He returned to the coroner's office and upon inquiring was told that both shoes were missing.

On his way back to Laynard, Moe stopped at the site of the accident and again searched both sides of the road, about one-half mile each way. He found nothing. He made a mental note that one of Roy Lee's shoes was missing.

Back at his office he found Louise reading a comic book with the usual wad of bubble gum in her mouth. "Any phone calls?" he asked.

"Just one. Mr. Welsh wants you to call him."

"What the hell does he want?" Moe said. "Get him on the phone."

"Hello. Edward Welsh here." Moe wondered why the voice irritated him so deeply. He knew it was because he had no respect for this weasel-like man with his nasal twang.

"This is Moe returning your phone call. What can I do for you?"

"I was just checking to see how our fine police force was handling things in Laynard."

"What do you mean?"

"Well, I was just wondering if you had identified or located the person that was involved in the hit-and-run accident that killed that young man yesterday?"

"No, but I'm working on it."

"Well, you get it cleared up fast. I don't want anything like that dragging on that might cast a bad light on activities at the rodeo."

Moe slammed the receiver down on the cradle of the telephone. Asshole, he thought, I'm faced with solving a vehicular homicide and all he's concerned about is his damn rodeo.

"Chief, you need a glass of iced tea to cool off a little bit," Louise said as she poured the lukewarm liquid over cubes she had taken from the icebox. "Have you found out who ran over that boy yesterday?"

"No, and I don't have any leads," he admitted. "But something will break before too long. Someone, somewhere has some pertinent information. It's just a matter of time." Moe hoped he was right.

I wonder if Joe saw anything? Louise thought. I'll have to remember to ask him the next time I see him.

Ten

The small simple casket, with an air of finality, was suspended above a large gaping hole dug in the ground. The pile of dirt at the side of the hole had been gracefully covered with a green colored carpet in an attempt to soften the harshness of the occasion. In the casket were the remains of the broken body of Roy Lee. He had been so mutilated that the undertaker had recommended that the casket not be open during the funeral. Mary had insisted that Roy Lee be buried in the new work pants she had bought for him as a present on the afternoon that he was killed. She didn't want him to be embarrassed at wearing bib overalls.

An ominous west wind whipped the tarp which had been hastily erected in anticipation of rain. Sobs and sounds of shuffling feet came from the small crowd of people standing behind the folding chairs where Al and Mary and the two grandparents sat. Six of Al's best friends acted as pallbearers and formed a semicircle at each end of the casket. They stood straight and tall like sentinels guarding the gates of eternity.

Mary noted the inscription on the small headstone of the adjacent grave: Helen: A treasure lies here. At least they would have company, she thought, brother and sister buried side by side in the cold ground. The grief of one tragedy should have been all that God required of you. Why had he demanded that she suffer two? Had she committed some sin so awful that God deemed justified such severe punishment?"

In the ensuing days after Roy Lee's death, Mary had cursed God. He was not just. He was not loving or kind as she had been told. Finding no meaning to life, she had wanted to die. How could death be worse than the suffering she had gone through losing two of her children? She had suffered so much in her relatively short life. Being the thirteenth child in a family that scratched out a living on a tenant farm, she had lived in poverty during her childhood. A brother and two sisters had died as she was growing up. Her father had died from a heart attack two months after Al and she were married. Her mother followed him to the grave less than a year later. The doctor said that she had died of a broken heart. Work and suffering seemed to be the recipe of life. Could the cycle ever be broken? Would there ever be a time in her life when she would be totally happy?

She heard the words of the minister: "The Lord giveth and the Lord taketh away… from dust to dust…" A feeling of guilt came over her. Sitting before the open burial pit she realized the awesome possibilities death presented. If life went on in a different dimension after death, were there any options? Was our present life a time of selecting the path we would take after death? A small voice whispered from her soul, "Forgive me, take care of Roy Lee and love him as I have."

Al focused on the single red rose he had placed on the casket. He had picked it from his father's rose garden. It had been but a bud last evening, but had opened up into a blossom early that morning. Now it would only wither and die, its beauty lasting for such a short time. How much Roy Lee was like that rose, taken at full bloom only to die and turn to dust.

Al refused to let tears fill his eyes. He blocked grief from the door of his heart. He would survive this tragedy. He had searched for reasons, but knew he could not find the answers. He had suffered guilt, feeling responsible, but realized that he had let Roy Lee pick up the mail many times before. What happened was life, and one had to find a way to survive the pain of living.

The crowd of people edged under the tarp as raindrops began to fall. Bright streaks of lightning danced across the sky. Dark ominous clouds banked the horizon. Moe Hendersen stood at the rear of the crowd, towering a head above most of the other people. He could see Mary and Al sitting on the folding chairs next to the casket. He thought of his own son. How could he ever stand the pain of losing him. His heart grieved for his best friend Al and Al's wife Mary.

The past three days had been hectic for Moe. He had gone over and over the information he had on the accident, but there weren't enough pieces and nothing fit together to give him any clue to what had happened. Numerous phone calls had proved futile. People had claimed they saw the car that hit the boy, but wouldn't give their names so that their statements could be confirmed.

Reports came in from the public indicating the color of the car that ranged from red to black to white. One person called in and said he had witnessed the accident and a motorcycle had been involved. Moe had spent hours following up on all these leads, but they all led to a blind alley. Every clue or piece of information had been painstakingly checked out. Nothing new had surfaced. He was no closer to solving the accident than he was the day it had happened.

Moe waited as most of the people darted to their cars between raindrops. Mary sat alone staring at the casket as Al assisted his parents to their car. "I'm so sorry," Moe said, as he laid a gentle hand on Mary's shoulder. "I wish there was something I could do to ease your grief. I know you will never forget him, but time will heal the pain. Come, let me help you to your car." She felt so frail as he put his arm around her waist and led her to the spot where Al had pulled the car up to the grave site.

"Thanks," said Al as Moe assisted Mary into the passenger's side of the car. "We really appreciate you coming to the funeral. It means a lot to both of us. Having a friend like you is important at a time like this."

Moe felt the sincerity in Al's voice and also noted the lack of grief. It was if Al had blocked it out, refusing to accept it, letting it be buried with his son. Moe wondered who would suffer the most in the coming weeks, Mary or Al. He said a silent prayer for both of them. "If there's anything I can do for you, be sure to let me know." Moe knew that the funeral was not the time or the place to question Al about the accident.

Maybe he would drive out to their house tomorrow or the next day to see if he could get Al to remember any more details. It appeared as if Al was the only eyewitness, so that was where he would have to concentrate his investigation.

Al arose early the next morning. After he had finished the chores, he sat quietly eating the cereal that Mary had fixed for him. Finishing, he abruptly stood up and gave Mary a peck on her cheek. "I have to mow the north pasture this morning," he said. "I'll be done by lunch time."

Mary watched him walk down the dirt path toward the barn. She knew it was impossible for him to share his pain with anyone. That was just his nature. He had refused to accept sympathy from everyone except his friend Moe. She hoped his hurting would ease. A noise startled her. Turning, she saw Gene at the top of the stairs.

"I w-want Roy Lee to c-come home so I c-c-can play with h-h-him," said Gene as Mary poured milk on his cereal. Mary bit her lower lip, trying to mask the pain in her heart.

"He's gone away to be with God."

"Does h-h-he w-want to be w-with God i-i-instead of us?" The question surprised Mary. She really hadn't thought of it in that vein. A person had no choice, no part in the decision of death. God commanded all the controls, giving man no options.

"...and h-h-he didn't e-even tell m-me good-by," Gene said.

"God must have loved him so much that he was in a hurry to have him come to heaven," Mary said, questioning her own beliefs.

Mary sat at the table with her hands covering her face. Would the incessant pain ever go away? Would sorrow ever ease? She reached for the old family Bible laying on a shelf that also held her wedding pictures and snapshots of the children. She blew the dust off the gilded edges of the pages. As the Bible fell open, she saw the words: "The Lord is the everlasting God, the creator of the ends of the earth. He will not grow tired or weary, and his understanding no one can fathom. He gives strength to the weary and increases the power of the weak."

She remembered the words her mother had said to her when she was a child: "God will never cause you to suffer more than the strength he gives you to overcome suffering." The whisper of God brushed her heart and a great weight was lifted from her soul. Mary felt the stirring of a new life in her body. Maybe God would give her another daughter after all.

The Laynard weekly newspaper was sticking obliquely out of the mailbox on the front door of his office as Moe arrived at work. Moe enjoyed the early morning hours in his office. It was usually fairly quiet around city hall at this time of day. It was a time he could get caught up on his reports or answer correspondence without any interruptions. He plugged in the small hot plate holding the battered old coffee pot Louise had filled the night before. The air in the office was heavy with humidity. Gonna be a hot one today, he thought as he turned on the floor fan. He grimaced at the noise it made.

Louise had neatly stacked the papers and journals on his desk. Two freshly sharpened number-two lead pencils laid beside a yellow legal pad. Yesterday's date had been torn off the calendar ring. Moe liked neatness and order. It complemented his meticulous approach to his work. This was the morning of the week he looked forward to, circulation day of the Laynard newspaper. He would spend thirty to forty minutes reading the publication from front to back while drinking two cups of coffee. It was seldom that there was much of interest, let alone anything earthshaking in its pages, but it was habit, part of his weekly routine. He inhaled deeply, savoring the aroma of the coffee as the old coffee pot danced on the redhot coil of the hot plate. Leaning back in his swivel chair, he placed his feet on an open drawer on the desk and unfolded the small newspaper. On the front page was a picture of Edward Welsh. Under the picture in dark bold print were the words: "RODEO EXECUTIVE CRITICIZES LOCAL CHIEF OF POLICE." Moe hurriedly scanned the article below the picture.

"...Mr. Welsh wonders if the chief of police of Laynard is effectively investigating an accident involving the death of a nine-year-old boy on the opening day of the rodeo. The accident happened a week ago and to date there are no leads as to who was responsible for the apparent hit-and-run accident. Welsh speculates that it was probably alcohol related. He also accuses the chief of being negligent in not setting up checkpoints to stem the flow of alcohol into our communities from the state line. Welsh states that he had recommended to the chief that a roadblock be set up south of Laynard on the afternoon of the accident to prevent alcohol from being brought to the rodeo performance. However, the chief didn't deem it necessary to do so. Welsh also said he had reports that at the time of the accident, the chief was sitting in his office having coffee with his wife."

Moe was considered to be a patient and gentle man, slow to anger, never getting upset no matter what the turn of events.

However, when anger was evoked he became a raging bull intent on avenging his anger with his great physical strength. Edward Welsh picked up the ringing telephone and instantly recognized the voice on the other end of the line.

"You son of a bitch!" screamed Moe into the phone. "If I could get my hands on you, I'd wring that scrawny neck of yours. You're the biggest two-faced bastard I've ever seen. Of all the times I've picked you up driving under the influence of alcohol and let you off with just a warning ticket. Don't think I don't know about the supply of illegal liquor you keep in the basement of your house and the parties you have involving teenagers. If I ever hear one more peep out of you about how I do my job, I'll haul you in and put you behind bars!"

Edward Welsh dropped the phone back on the desk. His face was cherry red. He swallowed hard as he wiped the beads of sweat from his brow. He realized he had gone too far. Moe was not the kind of person to be bullied. He shuddered, thinking what Moe might do to him physically if they ever came in contact.

Later that morning, Al let his team of mules drink their fill at the water tank before putting them in their stalls. It had taken him longer to mow the pasture than he had thought. Mary was probably wondering where he was. As he left the barn the familiar police car drove up the drive. "Hello, Moe," he said, wiping the sweat from his forehead with his shirt sleeves. "Hope this is just a social call, what with all that's been happening lately."

"Actually, I want to ask you some more questions about the accident if you don't mind."

"Don't mind, but I think I've told you everything I remember."

"I just want to be sure I haven't missed anything," Moe said.

When they shook hands Moe was taken back at the smell of alcohol on Al's breath. When they were younger they had done a lot of hard drinking together. However, after they were married and settled down, drinking became only a social activity and seldom did it involve more than a couple of drinks. What was Al doing drinking in the middle of the day during the week?

"Come on in and we'll talk while we have a bite to eat, and don't tell me you aren't hungry. I know how you can't resist good food."

Moe put up very little resistance when Mary offered him a piece of apple pie and coffee. Then he asked, "Al, can you remember any other cars going by just before or right after the accident?"

"No, not that I can remember."

"Have you had any luck trying to remember the type or color of the vehicle?"

"Well, I can't remember the type, but it could have been red. I'm not sure."

"I'm sorry, but I just can't remember any other details," Al said after several more questions from Moe. "Did you find Roy Lee's other shoe in your car?"

"What do you mean?" Al asked.

"Both of his shoes were missing when you got to the hospital, and I only found one at the scene of the accident."

"I haven't seen it," said Al. "I don't know where it could be."

"Do you think you'll ever find out who the driver of the car was?" Mary asked, as she cleared the empty plates from the kitchen table.

"I sure hope so, but it's taking a lot longer than I had expected."

"I would think that anyone with any morals or sense of justice would have come forward by now to confess. Surely whoever did it knows it was an accident," Mary said.

"That's what I thought," said Moe. "That makes me think we may be dealing with something more than a mere accident. Maybe the car was stolen. Maybe there were drugs in the car. It could be that it was a drunk driver. Anyway, something is bound to turn up sooner or later. I'll admit I'm a little frustrated that things are dragging out so long. I know you folks are anxious to find out who the guilty party is and to see justice done so you can get on with living."

"Don't let our friendship put any added pressure on you, Moe," Mary said. "I know that even though you may never find out who is responsible, if they did anything wrong they will be punished in their own way."

As Moe backed the patrol car out of the driveway, he thought about what Mary had said. Did a higher level of justice exist that went beyond the laws of man? A power that made sure that no bad deed went unnoticed, that punishment was meted out when justified? Moe's analytical mind could not rest comfortably with such a concept. He had to solve this case and if a crime had been committed, see to it that proper punishment was provided.

A garbage truck backed slowly toward the trash receptacle at the rear of the service station south of Carville. Two husky young men leaped from their riding positions on the rear bumper of the truck. In ballet-like movements they lifted the trash receptacle and emptied its contents into the back of the truck.

As they returned the receptacle to its original position, one of them noted an object that had been lying under the receptacle. Picking it up, he saw that it was a small work shoe. It looked almost new. "I wonder why anyone would throw away a perfectly good shoe?" he asked. "I wonder if I should turn it in to the gas station? Someone may be looking for it." Deciding not to, he threw the shoe into the back of the truck as he jumped back to his riding position on the rear bumper of the truck.

Eleven

The growing child in her body had helped to heal the sorrow she suffered from losing Roy Lee. Mary still thought of him every day, and at times would turn abruptly, anticipating his presence. Even though he was not physically there, their spirits would meet and the heartaches she had once suffered were replaced with pleasant memories of the happy times they had spent together. She would recall their strolls through the timber behind their house and his excitement in finding a wildflower. She could smell the scent on her fingers after they counted the petals of a wild rose. The wounds of grief had healed in her heart, leaving only a faint telltale scar as a reminder of the sorrow she had suffered.

She was concerned about Al. Since Roy Lee's death he had become very withdrawn. Many mornings he would get up early, fix his own breakfast and leave for the fields before she even got up. They seldom spoke to each other anymore. After supper he would go down to the barn, saying he had work to do. Most nights she would be in bed when he finally came in from working. Then she had begun to notice the alcohol on his breath.

Al finished milking the last of the short-horn cows. He missed the companionship of Roy Lee. No one knows how much a son means to a father unless he has lost one of his own, Al thought as he released the cows from their stalls. At first he had been able to bar grief from his heart, but as time went by, the jagged edges of sorrow tore through the barriers he had placed. Al took a paper sack off the shelf in the back of the milking shed. Removing the bottle of Old Crow, he unscrewed the cap and took a long drink. Grimacing as the hot liquid burned his esophagus on the way down, he replaced the bottle on the shelf. He knew this would help fend off the grief for a little while.

Mary sat the steaming plate of fried chicken on the kitchen table. "I fixed your favorite meal tonight," she said as she affectionately squeezed his shoulder.

"It was also Roy Lee's favorite," Al said in a defiant voice.

"I'm sorry, I didn't mean to bring back sad memories. Honey, I know you miss him, so do I, but we have to go on living. You have two other beautiful children that need your love. You haven't spent any time with them lately. I need you too. I feel so helpless. I wish there was something I could do to help you. I miss that old spark you used to have."

Guilt accentuated the power of the grief that was pounding at his heart. Al knew that he had neglected his family, especially his wife. He even felt selfish, being so intent on his own feelings that he ignored the feelings of those around him, those he loved. However, the ever-present grief laid in ambush, waiting for him to weaken. It took his total concentration and physical energy to ward it off. He was fearful of the pain he would suffer if it ever inflamed his heart. "I have to drive into town tonight," Al said, offering no explanation as to why.

"You want the kids and me to ride in with you?"

"No, I won't be long."

Mary watched, with mounting concern, as Al backed out of the driveway onto the dirt road. What could she do to soothe the agony he had experienced since Roy Lee's death? She prayed daily for God to grant him peace of mind and strength to cope with his fears. She loved him so much.

"How's school going, son?" Moe asked the six-year-old boy sitting at the table across from him.

"Aw, okay," the boy said as he spread an ample amount of grape jelly on a homemade roll.

"What do you mean, okay? Do you like your teachers?"

"They're okay." Moe Hendersen, Jr. was big for a six-year-old. The older he grew, the more his features resembled those of his adoptive father. In school he had the nickname "Little Ox." He was proud of the nickname because he often heard his father jokingly called "Big Ox" by his friends. He worshipped the ground his father walked on. His goal in life was to become a policeman just like his father.

He was elated the first day of school when his father drove him to school in the police car. As they pulled up to the front of the school, his father turned on the blinking red light on top of the car and blew the siren. All of his classmates had come running from the playground and surrounded the vehicle, making "oh" and "ah" sounds. He bubbled with pride. He had the best father in the world.

One day he suggested to his father that instead of going to school he could learn to be a policeman by spending the days riding with him in the police car. It was a waste of time to learn all those unimportant things they taught you in school.

"To be a good policeman, you have to learn to read and write and to think and reason," his father had told him. "So, if you want to be a policeman you will have to go to school and study real hard."

Relenting, Moe Jr. had accepted the fact that school was

a necessary evil he had to endure if he was going to be a good policeman like his father.

Moe waved at his son as he backed out of the driveway. "If you get your homework done by the time I get back from my night patrol, I'll play a game of Chinese checkers with you."

The main street of Laynard was almost deserted as Moe made the loop through the three-block business area. Four cars were parked in front of Harbon's Tavern. The tavern was a new business in town. The county had just voted to rescind the ordinance forbidding alcohol to be sold in public establishments. "Wonder what fine citizens of Laynard are drinking at this time of night during the week," thought Moe as he pulled into a parking space.

As he entered the door of the tavern the lonesome notes of the song "Honky-Tonk Angel" drifted from the jukebox at the rear of the dimly lit room. Instantly he recognized the nasal twang of the recording star Hank Williams. Two couples sat in the rearmost booth engaged in friendly conversation. They saluted him with raised glasses as he entered. Two younger men were sitting at the bar on either side of a middle-aged lady. The lady had made a vain attempt to look younger. Her bleached hair hung in long curls; a short, tight-fitting skirt exposed her fleshy thighs. On close inspection, the heavy layer of make-up intended to cover the lines of age gave her a ghostly look. The young men were vying for her attention, caressing her bare knees, then moving upward on the inner part of her thighs. She made a half-hearted attempt to resist them; then, spreading her legs, she let them go even higher. "She'll probably wear both of them out tonight," Moe chuckled to himself.

He turned to leave, then noticed the solitary figure sitting at the far end of the bar. He recognized his friend Al. "What the hell are you doing here at this time of night?" Moe asked as he heaved himself onto the bar stool next to Al.

"Hi, old buddy, let me buy you a drink," slurred Al.

"Can't, I'm on duty. Besides, you look like you've had enough for both of us tonight."

"You're probably right," said Al as he finished off the bottle of beer in front of him.

"In fact, I believe you've had too much. I doubt you could hit a bull in the ass with a bass fiddle right now, and I don't want any argument, I'm driving you home."

Al offered little resistance as Moe guided him the length of the barroom and out the front door. He passed out in the front seat of the patrol car before Moe could shut the door.

The dark clouds forming on the horizon were an omen of an impending storm. Mary squinted her eyes in the dim light of the kerosene lamp as she put new patches on the elbows of Al's work shirt. An insidious dread fell upon her. Where was Al? she wondered. What could be keeping him this long? He knew how she worried and usually let her know if he was going to be late. Had he been in an accident?

At first, she thought the noise was the sound of distant thunder. Then, as she saw the headlights reflect on the kitchen window, she realized it was a car coming up the driveway. An audible sigh of relief escaped her lips. She was startled by the knock at the door. Surprise framed her face as she opened the door and saw Moe in the doorway holding Al in an upright position. "What's happened?" she demanded.

"I believe he's had a tad too much to drink," said Moe as he winked and smiled at Mary. Moe laid Al on the sofa and placed a pillow under his head. "There, he'll sleep it off and be fine tomorrow."

"I'm so embarrassed," said Mary. "He hasn't gotten like this for years. What's come over him?"

"Everyone has to let off steam sometime," said Moe. "I wouldn't worry about it. Tomorrow he probably won't even remember what he did tonight."

"Thank you for driving him home. I shudder to think what might have happened if he had tried to drive himself."

"No trouble," said Moe as he squeezed Mary's hand. "He's my friend." Moe paused at the doorway and looked at Mary. Even with child she had a radiant beauty about her. Words formed on his lips, but instead of speaking he turned abruptly and left.

Outside, the thunderclouds darkened as Mary climbed the stairs to the bedroom. Al lay snoring on the sofa.

The house was quiet as Moe turned the key in the back door. The tumbling bolt echoed in the stillness of the night. A single light glared from a desk lamp. On the kitchen table was the Chinese checker board with all the marbles in place to play a game. Written on a piece of paper beside it was, "We'll play tomorrow night: I LOVE YOU, DAD."

Louise laid awake in her bed. Sleep had evaded her. Visions of Joe dominated her thoughts. His hands were exploring her body, his tongue caressing her breast. She could taste the sweat from his forehead. A moan of desire escaped her lips. It had been almost three weeks after they had made love at the old log cabin that he had called her late one evening, suggesting that they go for a ride.

At first she had refused, hurt that he had waited so long to call her. When he whispered over the phone what he would do to her, she quickly assented. They had parked on a dead-end country road east of Laynard near the bluffs. He had removed her clothes piece by piece, touching every part of her body, and then made love to her in the back seat of his car.

Afterwards, as she was putting her clothes back on, she had casually asked him if he had seen the accident that killed the nine-year-old boy on the afternoon they had made love at the log cabin. She was taken aback by his response. He had become irritated and irrational, saying he didn't know anything about the accident and didn't want her to ever mention it again. He had not called her since. She had last seen him about two weeks ago. He was putting gas in his car at the local self-service station. Walking up behind him, she pressed her body close to his. When he turned around to face her, she shrugged, letting the strap of her halter fall off her shoulder. It came dangerously close to exposing her nipple.

"Let me fill your tank with gas," she whispered in his ear.

"I have to get back to the office," he said. "I've got an appointment with a client."

"It won't take long, and besides, what client could be as important as having me make love to you?"

Joe parked the car in a clump of trees along a seldom traveled country road. She sensed that today she would have to be the aggressor. Before, Joe had been the one to initiate the activity, always with the intensity of a young stallion. This had given her the opportunity to be coy and tease him, rejecting his actions until he was in a frenzy. This day he seemed preoccupied, his thoughts somewhere else.

"I've been saving these for you," she said, unhooking her halter and exposing her firm breast. She pulled his head down to her nipple. He turned away. "What's wrong, honey?" she cooed as she began to rub his thigh.

"I just don't feel like doing it today."

"I'll help you," she said, unbuckling his belt. It was to no avail. She was not able to arouse him.

Twelve

At first Joe had tried to keep the accident buried in the deep, dark crevices of his mind. The vision of a child's body covered with blood kept coalescing in his thoughts. He couldn't remember seeing the boy at the time, but the latent image plagued him daily. It preoccupied him to the point that he was having trouble concentrating on his work.

The first few weeks after the accident he had forced himself to listen to the local news every night, fearful of hearing that he might be implicated. A secure feeling would come over him when nothing more was said about the incident, but the next day the fear would return just before news time. Paranoia set in. He knew that someone could identify him as the driver of the car that killed the boy. Why didn't people just come forth and accuse him? What were they doing? Were they toying with his mind, trying to drive him to mental madness? Louise must know. She had asked him about it. How could she know? Then Tad had all but accused him when he questioned the damage to the front of his car. Rosie knew. She kept baiting him, asking him where he had been that afternoon when he was supposed to be with Tad. The boy's father had been parked right across the road, the newspaper had said. Surely he saw what had happened. He probably even got his license plate number. What were they waiting for? Were they trying to drive him to the breaking point?

The pain started again behind his left eye, a piercing explosion of white-hot metal. The black spider of his dreams gloated at his terror as it fed on the guilt in his subconscious mind. With trembling hands he reached for the pain pills in his coat pocket.

The animal-like scream awoke Rosie from a deep sleep. She was in the middle of a dream where a handsome young man was guiding her around a ballroom. For a second she was disorientated, not wanting the dream to end. Then she realized that the scream came from Joe, lying in bed beside her. His nightmares were getting more frequent, sometimes more than once a night.

She placed her hand on his chest. It was hot and clammy with fever. What was happening to her husband? For the last three months he had been having dramatic mood swings. At one moment he would seem normal and coherent, then he would go into irrational rages as if demons had inhabited his mind. Rosie had suggested that he seek medical help, but he refused. He had called Dr. Macke's office to obtain refills for the pain medication.

A couple of weeks ago Dr. Macke's nurse called Rosie, asking if she was aware that Joe had spilled his last refill of medication down the drain in the bathroom sink. "Yes," she had lied, not thinking of the implications. That evening, when she had questioned Joe about how much medication he was taking, he went into one of his rages. His eyes were bloodshot the next morning when he sat down at the breakfast table. His hair was uncombed and he had put on the same wrinkled shirt he had worn the day before.

"Why don't you take the day off and stay home and rest?" Rosie suggested.

"I'm behind in work at the office as it is. My boss told me that if I didn't get squared away he might have to let me go. Then you would have to get off your fat ass and go to work," he snarled.

As soon as Joe left for work, Rosie placed a call to Dr. Macke.

"Hello, Rosie, you're calling awful early in the morning. I hope nothing serious has come up."

"It's about Joe. I'm worried about him. He's been acting so strange lately."

"I've been going to call you. He's been calling the office frequently requesting refills on his pain medication. I'm afraid he may be getting addicted to them. I've got to refuse him any more requests for refills. I wanted you to know so you could contact me if he tried to get any medications from someone else."

"What's causing his pain?" Rosie asked.

"I don't really know. He hasn't been in for a complete examination for some time, but I suspect it could be something psychological. Of course, that's just an old GP's guess. Why don't you see if you can get him to go to the state hospital up at Lamars. They have specialists there who could give him a thorough going-over and if it is psychological, they can treat him better there."

"I doubt that I can talk him into going on his own. You know how stubborn he is."

"Well, if you're really worried about him I can sign the papers to get him admitted for psychological evaluation. Legally they can keep him fourteen days. You don't have to make the decision right now, but it's something to think about."

The day passed slowly for Rosie, and that night she tossed and turned, unable to sleep. Questions tortured her mind. Her thoughts raced for answers. Was Joe really mentally sick? Was she the cause of his problem? Did she have any choice but to commit him? Later that night, when Joe began sobbing in his sleep and mumbling about black spiders eating his body, she knew what she had to do.

Two weeks later, on a Monday morning, Joe was transported to the state hospital by a deputy assigned to the Department of Health and Human Welfare. He rode all the way in the back seat of a state car restrained in a straightjacket.

The newest magazine in the rack was over a year old, dog-eared, and with pages missing. The waiting room was crowded with people. There was only standing room in the smoking area.

Rosie lit up her sixth cigarette off the butt of the preceding one. As she blocked out the voices of those around her, she remembered how violent Joe had become when she suggested that he be examined at the state hospital. When they served papers on him to have him committed, he had screamed at her, telling her that he wanted her out of his house and never to set foot in it again. It pained her to see him so angry at her, but she knew there was no choice. Her husband needed help.

The nurse at the reception desk caught Rosie's eye and motioned for her. Rosie picked her way through the crowd. Stale cigarette smoke partially concealed the reek of human perspiration in the crowded room. "Dr. McCall can see you now," the nurse said. "Go down the hall on the right until you come to an exit sign. Dr. McCall's office is the fourth door on the right; just walk right in when you get there."

In bold letters on the door was, DR. McCALL: PSYCHIATRIST. Rosie was surprised as she entered the room at how young the man behind the desk was. His face was square, framed with unruly blond hair. His ice-blue eyes were magnified by the dark horn-rimmed glasses he wore.

The intensity of his gaze was softened by a radiant smile. Extending his hand to her, he said, "You must be Rosie. Your husband Joe has mentioned you several times in our discussions."

Won't you please have a seat?

"I understand you live a few miles east of Carville. That's where the big rodeo event is held every year, isn't it? I would sure like to find time to drop down some year and attend it."

Picking up a manila folder on his desk, he said, "We have given your husband Joe a rather thorough physical and psychiatric exam during the past four days. He seems to be in an excellent state of physical health for a man in his late thirties. However, from a psychological standpoint, he varies somewhat from normal expectancies. He is on the borderline of being manic-depressive with a deeply rooted guilt complex."

Confusion clouded Rosie's mind. She sensed that what Dr. McCall was telling her was serious, but she couldn't comprehend why her husband Joe should have all these exotic-sounding problems. "Can anything be done to make him well again?"

"I have proposed two approaches to treatment. First, I would recommend analysis. This is where we try to find out the cause of his guilt feelings. Somewhere, at some time, he must have suffered a severe traumatic insult to his psyche which he has tried to erase from his memory. If we can identify this, we may be able to bring it back to his conscious mind and help him deal with it on a day-to-day basis. We might be successful with this modality of treatment or we might not. If we are not successful, I would then recommend electric shock treatments."

Dr. McCall noticed Rosie cringe at the mention of electric shock treatments. "These are not as bad as most people think," he continued. "We have had excellent results with this treatment on some of our patients.

"We have diagnosed your husband as being unable to make decisions for himself. Since you are next of kin, we need your signature on a release form to give us authority to proceed with treatment."

It was impossible for Rosie to collate all of her thoughts. She knew Joe needed help, but this was an immense responsibility for her to take. She hoped Joe would understand when he recovered.

"I'll sign the papers," she said. "Can I see him now?"

"I'm sorry, but we have strict regulations forbidding patients to have any visitors during the initial diagnosis and evaluation sessions."

Joe hadn't received any medication that morning. Dr. McCall wanted him to be free of any mind-altering effects the drugs might have.

"Joe, I'm here to help you. I want to free you from this plague that is making your life unbearable. I need your cooperation. I cannot do it without your help. Will you do the things I ask you to do, even though they may be painful at first, but are necessary if we are going to help you?"

"Sure, I'll try." The words echoed in Joe's mind as if someone else had said them.

"Good. I want you to listen very closely to what I ask you to do," Dr. McCall said in a monotone voice. "You may not be able to do it but just think about doing it. I want you to take a deep breath...hold it till I count to three...one...two three...now slowly let it out. Do that again on your own...holding your breath for three counts...then letting it out all the way. Good, continue doing that, and as you breath out notice the relaxed feeling that spreads throughout your chest. Notice how this relaxed feeling spreads to your arms...to your shoulders...up your neck...downward into your legs...to your feet...to the very tips of your toes. Notice how your whole body becomes relaxed." Continuing the hypnotic induction technique, Dr. McCall was confident that Joe had entered a trance state. His breathing became deep and rhythmic. His head drooped forward until his chin was on his chest. His eyes were closed, his shoulders sagged and his hands laid limp in his lap.

"Joe, it is possible to go backward in time to places where we can remember everything we said, heard, felt, tasted, and even smelled. We can do this by thinking about taking a book and flipping the pages backward...going back to the beginning... or by moving the hands of a clock backward...backward to an earlier time. I want you to do this now...go back to the beginning by turning the hands of the clock backward. As you go backward you will remember the things that made you sad or hurt you...things you had no control over...It may be painful to remember these events, but they will become very vivid to you and you will tell me about them."

Dr. McCall made numerous notes on his pad of yellow paper as Joe's mind went backwards in time, describing events that had been in memory for many years. Father spent time in jail when patient was very young...Mother turned to prostitution...has vivid pictures of mother's sexual activity with strangers...numerous events that promoted feelings of abandonment...father never returned after serving time in jail...trouble with father-in-law...divorced first wife...promiscuity.

The doors of darkness were opened in Joe's mind, exposing the alcoves of pain and guilt. His life passed before him like a wide-screen movie. One door remained closed, held tight by the black spider refusing to be exposed, jealously guarding its secret. There were no references made in Dr. McCall's notes to the car accident where the young boy was killed.

Two weeks later, Dr. McCall reviewed all the clinical notes in the hospital record before him. Numerous traumatic events had surfaced from the past during the patient's session of age regression. Any of these events held the potential to effect one's mental health. After each event had been discussed in detail with the patient, it was impossible to isolate the etiology of the trauma causing the present mental state. "Is there something I've missed?" Dr. McCall wondered aloud. "Is there something so deeply seated that it hasn't surfaced during my analysis?"

Dr. McCall finished filling out the discharge summary in Joe's hospital record. He had written a recap in abbreviated form of his evaluation and diagnosis. Under the heading "Recommendation:" he wrote, "Release patient to care of his wife. Medications: Lithium carbonate 300 mg. tid, Thorazine 10 mg tid. Inpatient reevaluation in 30 days to establish serum levels of medication. If symptoms persist, will consider electroshock therapy at a later date."

Rosie smiled at the security guard stationed at the entrance to the psychiatric ward. "No smoking on the ward," he said, as she pulled the package of cigarettes from her purse. She had just left Dr. McCall's office. She was excited to see Joe again. She had not been permitted to see him for the fifteen days he had been incarcerated at the state hospital. Dr. McCall had cautioned her that Joe might appear a little slow and unsure of himself due to the tranquilizing effect of the medication that he was on. He had also warned her to try to keep Joe in an atmosphere that was as stress-free as possible. She was instructed to report any reoccurrence of the nightmares or any unusual behavior. He stressed the importance of maintaining the medication schedule.

"Does that mean that he won't have to have those electric shock treatments?" she had asked.

"Maybe," he had answered in an unconvincing tone. Joe had on the shirt, tie, and dress pants she had dropped off the day before. He chatted with the orderly at his side as he entered the waiting room. Rosie's heart quickened when he smiled and came toward her with his arms open.

"I'm so glad to see you, honey," Rosie said, hugging him tightly. Sensing his unsteadiness, she took his arm as they left.

"How do you feel?" she asked as she backed out of the parking lot.

"I'm glad to be out of that place. It's sorta scary, all the questions they keep asking you. Some of the people in there are really crazy. I even think some of the employees working there should be patients."

His manner was docile, his movements slow and precise. There was a light slur to his speech. Gone was the angry rage which had besieged him the last few months. Maybe the medication will work, thought Rosie. Gone too was the Joe she once knew—the cocky young man that had swept her off her feet with his macho attitude, the lover that sexually never seemed to tire of her.

"I wonder if he will want to make love to me when we get home?" she mused.

Thirteen

The infant eagerly attached herself to the milk-laden breast. The hungry little mouth made loud sucking noises until it was properly positioned. Mary looked down with contentment at her two-month-old daughter. God had blessed her. She had prayed that the child she was carrying would be a girl. Mary had also prayed for God's presence with Al to ease his suffering. It was as if Al was afraid to accept Roy Lee's death, afraid of the sorrow he would have to endure. God had not answered this prayer.

Tears filled Mary's eyes as she thought about the events of the last few months. Early on she had overlooked the fact that Al was drinking. She rationalized that it was his way of managing his grief. As time passed his drinking became more frequent. It got to the point where he spent about every weeknight in town, sitting by himself at the bar in the local tavern, drinking beer until closing time. It was customary for the whole family to drive into Laynard every Saturday evening. Groceries for the coming week were purchased. The remainder of the evening was either spent in the local cinema or on the sidewalks socializing with other farm families.

There were those individuals in the community who spent Saturday evening in the local tavern, playing cards and drinking. Al started joining this group, letting Mary take the kids with her to purchase the supplies they needed, while he cavorted with his newfound friends in the tavern.

Mary recalled the numerous times she sat waiting for him in the car with Gene and Jimmy asleep in the back seat. Many Saturday nights it would be midnight before he left the tavern. Sometimes he would have trouble finding the car on the deserted street. He always refused her offer to drive even though many times he shouldn't have been behind the wheel. One Saturday night, late in her pregnancy, she became ill while she waited in the car for him. She had never gone into the tavern to get him before. She would have been too embarrassed to enter such a place. This night, though, feeling so sick, she decided that she had to go in and get him to take her home.

The loud blare of the jukebox pounded in her ears as she opened the tavern door. The reek of cigarette smoke increased her nausea. Al turned to see who had placed a hand on his shoulder. When he saw it was Mary, he said roughly," What the hell do you want?"

"Got her pregnant and barefoot again, eh, Al?" sneered one of the men sitting close by. A chuckle arose from the crowd around the table.

Mary flushed with embarrassment. "I don't feel good, please come and take me home."

"As soon as I finish this beer," he said, lifting a half-filled bottle from the table. "You go on and wait in the car. I'll be right there."

She had been waiting about fifteen minutes when she saw

the police car pull into the adjacent parking lot.

"You're in town kinda late, aren't you, Mary?" said Moe as she rolled down her window. "Don't tell me Al is still in there drinking beer."

Mary couldn't hold back the sobs. "Yes, and I told him fifteen minutes ago that I didn't feel good and wanted to go home."

Moe felt the hair bristle on the back of his neck. Mary didn't deserve this. No wife did, especially if she was pregnant. "I'll go in and get him," said Moe.

"No, I don't want you to get involved in our family problems. Anyhow, he would probably get angry, and I don't want you to do anything that might harm your friendship with him."

"Well, the least I can do is take you and the kids home."

"I'd appreciate that."

The house was wrapped in darkness as Mary and Moe entered the back door. Moe had picked up Gene and Jimmy from the back seat of the car and carried them, one under each arm.

"It's times like this that I wish we could afford to have electricity put in the house," said Mary as she fumbled for a matchstick on the wood range. The yellow light of the kerosene lamp cast a soft glow throughout the room. Lifting the lamp above her head, Mary led the way up the stairs. Moe gently laid Gene and Jimmy on the bunk beds in the room on the left at the top of the stairs.

"I feel better already just being home," said Mary as they descended the stairs. "I want to thank you, Moe, for bringing us home. You're a very dear friend."

Try as he might, Moe could not understand what was wrong with his friend Al. What had caused this drastic change in attitude? Moe had attempted to talk to him as a friend, but Al had refused to listen to him. It was as though there was an unwritten code in their friendship; discussion of one's marital problems was taboo. The problem weighed heavily on Moe's mind. These were his two closest friends.

Moe noted the silhouette of her body, formed by the rays from the kerosene lamp. She makes a beautiful pregnant lady, he thought. As she turned, he placed his hands on her waist. She reached up and clasped his shoulders. The shadows covered the adoration in her eyes. "I love you, Moe, in a very special way," she murmured as she laid her head on his chest.

He smelled the fragrance in her hair. He kissed her tenderly on the forehead. "If you ever need anything or someone to talk to, you know I'll always be there for you," he said with heated emotion. They lingered momentarily, relishing the sensation of contact between their bodies. Reluctantly they moved apart from the embrace.

Mary had confronted Al numerous times about his drinking. He cut her short, saying that she was overreacting. Out of love she tried reasoning with him, attempting to make him sensitive to the stress he was putting on their marital relationship. Al refused to listen to her, saying that her complaining was doing more harm to their marriage than his drinking. Slowly, the strong and happy ties they had once shared together as a family began to deteriorate.

"C-c-can I h-h-hold h-her after s-s-she's finished nursing?" asked Gene. He adored his new baby sister. He enjoyed watching the expressions on her face. When she was mad it would wrinkle up like a prune before she let out a shrill scream. When she was contented she would coo like the pigeons that roosted in the barn and her face would take on an angelic appearance.

When Mary brought the baby from the hospital she asked Gene what he wanted to name his new baby sister. "I w-w-want to c-c-call her 'Shirley' like the g-girl in the b-b-book," he said. "So she'll be b-b-brave and s-strong." In the story book, Shirley was a young girl who had heroically saved her family from a house fire. It was his favorite story. He never tired of hearing Mary read it. He was tickled when they christened the baby Shirley Mae. He was also very proud—he could say her name without stuttering.

"There, you can try to make her burp," said Mary, as she laid the baby on the towel she had placed on his shoulder.

Gene gently stroked the back of the little baby as she

gurgled contentedly in his arms. "W-w-when is d-d-daddy going to c-come and see us and Shirley?" he asked his mother.

A tide of guilt and anger ebbed through Mary's heart. She would never forget the evening Shirley was born. It was a cold and rainy fall evening. Al had left her and the two boys at home to spend the evening at the tavern drinking with his friends. She had begged him to stay home. She knew that her time to deliver was near and she had a premonition it would be that evening. Al said that he wouldn't stay late and left her crying in despair.

The contractions started about nine o'clock that evening just as the blunt force of the rainstorm hit. The thunder woke Gene, and she had let him stay up to keep her company.

"W-what's w-w-wrong, Mom?" he asked as the second wave of contractions caused her to gasp.

"I think the baby's coming!"

"Will d-d-daddy get h-h-home in time to t-take you to the h-h-hospital?"

"He promised he would," said Mary hopefully. As the contractions began to increase in frequency and intensity, Mary began to panic. They had talked about having a telephone put in for the last six months, but had put it off because Al said they didn't have enough money. He had become very angry when she suggested that they could have easily paid for a phone in a month with the money he spent on his drinking. She worried about having an emergency arise and not being able to summon help. She contemplated having Gene walk to the neighbor's house to seek help, but because of the storm she didn't want him out on that dark road so late at night.

Al arrived home about midnight that night. As he came staggering in the door, she screamed at him, "I'm having the baby! You have to get me to the hospital!" Turning to Gene, she said, "You'll have to be my big helper now. You must stay here and take care of Jimmy while your father takes me to the hospital. He'll come right back as soon as he gets me there."

Mary was petrified as Al raced down the country road, weaving from side to side, barely missing the drainage ditches on each side. Twice she had to grab the wheel to prevent him from going off the road.

As soon as she was settled in a bed in the emergency room, she sent Al back to the house to be with the two boys. Dr. Kern walked into the room just as the baby's head was emerging. He quickly removed his raincoat and took the place of the nurse at the end of the bed. Mary faintly remembered a shrill cry as Dr. Kern lifted the wriggling infant up for her to see, saying, "You have a healthy baby daughter!" Mary then drifted off into a deep, relaxed sleep.

Early the next morning, Mary called her older sister who lived with her family in Morgan Creek, about fifty miles east of Laynard. Ruth could sense the tears in her sister's voice when she asked, "Can you drive down and pick up Gene and Jimmy and keep them at your house while I'm in the hospital?"

"We would love to have the boys stay with us," said Ruth, wondering why Al couldn't take care of them. "I can leave in about fifteen minutes. I'll stop at the hospital after I pick them up and visit with you a few minutes, and check out that new daughter."

Ruth arrived at the house that morning to find Gene and Jimmy fixing their own breakfast. Al was lying on the sofa, still hung over from his drinking the night before. She was at a loss for words. She had never seen him in such a state. He was unshaven and reeked of alcohol. She quickly packed a bag with some clean clothes for the boys and left.

Gene ran ahead of Jimmy and his Aunt Ruth toward the front entrance of the hospital. "Hurry," he said over his shoulder. "I want to see the baby!"

Standing at the edge of the bed, he was eye level with the small figure lying in his mother's arms. "She's b-beautiful!" he exclaimed. "W-w-when c-can we take h-her h-h-home?"

"We have to wait until she gets stronger," his mother answered.

Ruth noted the tension in Mary's voice. "Anything you want to talk about?"

"Maybe later."

Al came to the hospital late in the afternoon the following day. He had been drinking since midmorning. As soon as he arrived he began flirting with the young nurse. He teased her about a hickey she had on her neck and how he would like to put a matching one on the other side. Mary remembered how embarrassed she had been. She told him to leave and not to come back until he was sober. He never returned to the hospital to see her or his daughter.

Dr. Kern scanned the hospital record as he entered Mary's room. "Seems like mother and daughter are doing just fine," he said. "I think you'll be able to take your new daughter home tomorrow. You can tell your husband that he can come and get you anytime after I make rounds in the morning."

Mary had slept very little the previous few nights. Some decisions had to be made. She tried to cope with Al's change in personality and make exceptions for his actions. How much longer could she go on under the strain and tensions of the past few months? She could sense the effect it was having on the two boys, and now with a new baby it would probably be worse. It had been a relief the last few days not having Al around. She didn't want to go home.

She made her decision. Calling her sister Ruth, she briefly described the situation with Al and asked if she could bring the baby to her house for a week or two until she could decide what to do.

Her sister seemed excited. "Mary, we'd love to have you visit us. We'll set up our extra bed in the basement and the neighbors have a crib that I'm sure we can borrow."

On the way to Ruth's house in Morgan Creek, Mary confided in her sister of the trouble between Al and herself. "I just don't see how things can ever be the same again," she sobbed.

"I'm sure you two can work out your problems if you just give it time. The relationship you had before was so strong, and it was evident that you both loved each other. I don't think anything that beautiful can ever be destroyed."

Two months had slipped by since she left the hospital. Her

sister's family had accepted them with open arms. The two sons, who were fourteen and sixteen, had adopted Jimmy and Gene, treating them as younger brothers. They taught Gene to ride a bicycle and pulled Jimmy in their little red wagon wherever they went. Ruth's husband had insisted that she stay with them when she had mentioned looking for an apartment.

Al called once, asking when she was coming home. She told him not until he quit drinking and began acting like a father and husband again. He had hung up on her.

"I g-g-got her to b-b-burp!" Gene said excitedly. "Now she can take her nap."

Mary basked in the warm comfortable setting of the basement room in her sister's house. It was such a happy, cozy place. They were having such a pleasant time there, but something was missing. At night, while lying in bed, she would ache for the touch of Al's hand, the feel of heat from his body. She missed his mischievous smile with his two gold front teeth. Would things ever again be like they were before?

Mary realized that she would have to make some decisions soon. She couldn't stay with her sister's family forever, even though they indicated she and the children could stay as long as they liked. The thought of leaving frightened her. How could she ever manage on her own with three children? Where would the money come from? There were so many questions that she had no answers for. That night she prayed to God for strength. She also prayed for Al.

Fourteen

Moe grimaced at his cluttered desk. Louise had taken two weeks off for vacation. The paperwork was piling up on him. Numerous records needed to be filed. A stack of unopened mail acted as a centerpiece for the large wooden desk. Systematically he began sorting through the mess. He was making progress until he picked up a file and noted the label in the upper left-hand corner: Identification #336, Subject—Vehicular Homicide. Roy Lee's name was written lengthwise on the edge of the file.

The file had remained on the top of his desk every day since the accident. It was a priority in his daily scheduling. No matter how busy he was or what he was doing, if any information came in concerning the accident, he would drop whatever he had been doing and check it out.

He contacted the State Bureau of Investigation, asking for their assistance in solving the case. An agent had come to his offic, reviewed the information he had on file, and then left. He hadn't heard from them again. No new information had come in for months. He was baffled by the fact that apparently no one witnessed the accident except Al. The information that Al gave him had been very limited and failed to provide any facts that would suggest a direction for further investigation. This was a fear that haunted most enforcement personnel, the fear of the failure to solve a crime. It was Moe's belief that every crime could be solved. It just depended upon the expertise of the investigating person to locate the missing pieces. As he studied the file, an intense feeling of failure enveloped him. "What did I miss?" he murmured to himself. It was bad enough to fail as a professional, but he also felt as though he had let down his best friend Al. If it had been his own son, would he have done anything different?

He refilled the stained coffee cup from the thermos he brought from home. The old hot plate in his office had heated its last pot of coffee two weeks ago. He had plugged it in to warm a pot of coffee, and the heating element had shorted out, exploding sparks like a Roman candle. There hadn't been any funds left in the city's bank account, so the city council denied his request for a new hot plate. He had jokingly suggested that the members of the city council take up a collection out of their own pockets and purchase him an automatic coffee maker. A good-humored uproar had ensued. "Then we'd have to let your secretary go because about the only work she does is make coffee for you," joked one of the councilmen. "That and stand around looking sexy," said another.

"She sure does a good job of that—making coffee, I mean," Moe had quipped. He was anxious for Louise to return from her vacation. She wasn't too bright, but she was dependable, always on time, and did her job. Also, she did add a little spice to his otherwise drab office. Occasionally, he even permitted himself the privilege of fantasizing about making love to her.

He sorted the items on his desk into three stacks. Each had a variety of different-sized pieces of paper. One pile, which was the largest, he picked up and dropped into the trash can beside his desk. The second pile he placed on top of the file cabinet to await filing until Louise returned. The third pile, correspondence he had to answer, he placed in a neat manner in the upper left-hand corner of the desk. Another item still remained on his desk: Roy Lee's file. He stared at it a few minutes; then reluctantly, he opened the bottom drawer of the file cabinet and placed it in the "Unsolved" file. It was almost like admitting defeat. Like being judged incompetent.

Joe swatted at two pesky flies that were buzzing around his forehead. His speed could not match their agility, and they droned away, alighting safely on the porch railing. Joe had gone back to work only half days, usually mornings, since his stay at the state hospital. When he got home at noon today, Rosie had taken the car into town to go shopping and run some errands. He moved his recliner out to the back porch so he could bask in the afternoon sun.

The warm sun rays penetrated his body, relaxing his muscles. Through half-closed eyes, he focused on the two flies on the porch railing. They made quick, short, darting movements on the painted surface of the wood railing. As if on cue, they ascended in flight, maneuvering like fighter planes in combat. Their erratic flight path made no sense to Joe as he tried to follow their movements.

Suddenly one of the flies stopped in midair. It seemed to be suspended in space. It's small body struggled in convulsions. Joe was perplexed. He focused his eyes and then he saw it, a huge spider web hanging from the ceiling at the corner of the porch. He watched with curiosity as life slowly ebbed from the small struggling fly.

A rush of blood filled his veins as he saw the black spider drop down from the darkness of the eaves. He had seen that spider before, with its eyes of many facets, but where? It seemed like a long time ago, but yet so near. The sun rays, cut off by the corner of the house, could not dispel a chill in the shadows on the back porch. Joe shivered as he drifted off into sleep. The spider lurked quietly, observing its prey.

Rosie found Joe asleep on the back porch when she returned late in the afternoon from shopping. She decided not to awaken him until she had supper prepared. It was good for him to relax and he wasn't due to take any medication for awhile.

Joe's boss had been very cooperative and understanding. Rosie confided in him regarding Joe's psychiatric evaluation. He left it up to Rosie as to what they felt was the best for Joe. Last week they had returned to the state hospital for Joe's first thirty-day evaluation. Joe's blood test showed that the blood serum level of the medication was within an acceptable range.

Rosie had been very optimistic answering Dr. McCall's questions. She told him that Joe hadn't had that terrible nightmare since he had been on the medication. She was concerned about how tired the medication made him, and how slow he seemed to move at times. "When can he stop taking the medication?" she asked.

"He may have to take the medication for the rest of his life. Since he seems to be doing reasonably well at the current dosage, I don't want to change it. We'll see how he gets along for the next thirty days," the doctor had said.

Meatloaf was on the menu for supper. It was one of Joe's favorite meals. She had thought about getting a bottle of red wine to go with the meal, but decided not to. Dr. McCall advised her that Joe should not drink any alcoholic beverages because of the medication he was on. She did miss those evenings, which seemed so long ago, where they would have cocktails before they ate, then share a bottle of wine during the meal.

"I might as well catch the early evening news while supper is cooking," she thought. She reached for a cigarette as the TV screen came to life. The package she pulled out of the pocket on her apron was empty. "I couldn't have smoked two packs already today." She went to the cupboard and opened a new carton.

"It's time for supper," she said, arousing Joe from a deep

sleep. "Did you spend all afternoon sleeping?"

"Yes, I was tired. I saw the spider," he muttered. "It killed a fly."

Fear gripped her. Had his nightmare returned?

The face in the mirror was a stranger to Al. How long had it been since he had shaved? Blurred memories of the past few weeks flashed through his mind. Most of the time he had spent in the tavern drinking with his newfound friends. They would play games where they would challenge each other to chug-a-lug a quart bottle of beer. The loser would have to pay for the next round.

He didn't remember ever losing. Many mornings he woke up not remembering driving home the night before. One night a buxom young lady sat on his lap. She giggled when he had unbuttoned her blouse and squeezed her firm breasts. As closing time neared he had asked if he could take her home. She refused, saying her boyfriend wouldn't like it if she went to bed with another man. He tried to remember her name but couldn't.

He noted the abrasion on his cheek. Last night the inevitable had happened. About midnight, on his way home from town, he drove his car off the road into a drainage ditch. He hadn't been hurt, just a bump on his forehead and a small laceration on his cheek. A passerby stopped and insisted that he go to the hospital to be checked out for any severe injuries.

Dr. Kern had not been too happy to be called into the emergency room at 12:30 at night, especially to examine a drunk that had run off the road. He cleaned the abrasion on Al's cheek and placed a bandage over it. "There's no need to keep you over night. I don't know what to do with you," he said, "but you're in no shape to send home by yourself." He hesitated to call the chief of police at that time of night, but felt he had no other choice.

The ringing of the telephone was amplified by the quiet of the night. Moe looked at the clock on the table next to the bed as he reached for the receiver; it read 1:15. He suddenly became fully alert. A call at this time of night was usually an emergency of some type.

"This is Dr. Kern," came the voice on the other end of the line. "I think you'd better come down to the emergency room. Your buddy Al has been in an accident."

"Is he hurt?"

"No, he's just drunker than a skunk and I don't know what to do with him."

Moe and Al rode in silence as they drove north on highway 65. The accident and the hot cup of black coffee the nurse had given him was beginning to have a sobering effect on Al. "Thanks for bringing me home," said Al, as Moe pulled up to the farmhouse. As Al turned to open the car door, Moe fiercely grabbed his forearm. There was anger in his eyes.

Moe took a deep breath, trying to find the words he wanted to say. "We used to be friends, but I haven't considered you a friend since the day you forced Mary to take the kids and leave you because of your drinking. Now I don't know what's bugging you, but you are taking the chance of losing the most precious wife one could ever ask for. For as long as I've known you, you have always had things your way. Always the top dog in the pack, arrogant and cocky. Well, it's time you grow up and think about someone other than yourself. Most people would be happy to have what you are throwing away. I'm done letting you off the hook. The next time I find you drunk in Laynard, I'm throwing you in jail for disturbance of the peace. Now, get your ass out of my car."

Moe drove home and slipped quietly into bed. "Anything serious?" his wife said in a sleepy voice.

"I may have just lost my best friend."

Al looked back at the image in the mirror. Moe's words kept echoing in his ears. "The most precious wife..." He continued to stare at the image in the mirror. Who am I? What have I done? he thought. A turbulence of guilt exploded within him.

His brain, ravaged by the effects of the alcohol the night before, rebelled as he tried to focus on reality. Try as he might, he could not dismiss the thoughts of possibly losing his family forever. He could not ever remember crying before. The torrent of sobs came from deep within him, wracking his body with convulsions. In his hand he clutched a framed photograph of Roy Lee.

The sobbing dismantled the barriers he had placed around his heart and permitted grief to enter. The sorrow he had feared engulfed him in a fiery hell. The pain ebbed ever so slowly and healing began. He looked at the photograph still clutched in his hand. "I will always love you and miss you," he said, "but now I must go on." Twenty-four hours later he stirred and awoke from a deep sleep. It was a new day.

Moe was startled when he saw Al waiting in the hallway in front of the door to his office. He looked almost human, clean-shaven and wearing an unsoiled white dress shirt with the cuffs rolled up.

"Good morning," Al said. "I decided I want to keep you as a friend. Can you drive me up to Morgan Creek today so I can visit Mary and the boys, and of course see my new daughter?"

"Sure can; in fact I can leave right now."

Fifteen

"It's your son Tad," said Rosie, handing the phone to Joe.

"Hi, Dad, I haven't seen you for such a long time I decided to give you a call and see how you are doing."

"I'm doing pretty good, only working half days till I get my strength built up. That damn medicine I have to take makes me so sleepy."

"What did the doctor have to say when you went back for your checkup at the hospital last week?"

"Well, he seemed to think I was doing pretty good. My blood tests came out okay. He's keeping me on the same medication. How are you getting along in your senior year at school?"

"I made the honor roll the first semester and I was elected class president."

"That's great, son. I always said you were a chip off the old block. When are you going to come over for a visit?"

"Maybe some afternoon next week after school when I don't have to work."

Joe looked forward to seeing his son again. He had only talked to him twice over the phone since the rodeo, and that was over eight months ago. He felt a strong bond to his son. This was his own flesh and blood. Since Rosie couldn't have children, it was left up to Tad to carry the family name into future generations. It had bothered Joe that Tad didn't have the traits most fathers look for in their sons. He was shy and timid. He would rather read or paint than play a game of sandlot baseball. He had characteristics which, in Joe's youthful days, would have been considered feminine in nature and would have earned the name Sissy. Had Tad inherited these traits from him through his genes? Was the absence of a father in the home during his early development responsible for the personality that had ensued? Somehow Joe felt guilty and responsible.

He had tried to be a good father. The hunting and fishing trips he planned with Tad, so they could be alone together, had all failed. Tad cried the first time he saw his father shoot a rabbit. He threw his fishing pole in the water after watching Joe tear a hook out of the mouth of a small bluegill. Finally, Joe accepted the fact that Tad could not knowingly do anything that would cause any living creature to suffer harm.

The attempt to teach Tad any type of sports had been a fiasco. Any little scratch or bump he received would send him into the house crying to his mother. Joe would get so exasperated and angry that he would tell him he was a baby and should play with the little girls.

Joe always felt depressed after these episodes of trying to be a good father. Why didn't Tad appreciate what he was trying to do for him? Even though Tad's mother and he were divorced, he was willing to try to be a father, unlike his own father, who had abandoned his mother and him when he was very young.

Maybe he will turn out all right after all, Joe thought. Making the honor roll and being elected class president your senior year was nothing to sneeze at. He might turn out to be a chip off the old block after all.

The eighteen-year-old boy had grown into a handsome, fine-featured young man. Tad excelled in his junior and senior years in high school. The teaching staff at Laynard High School had come to respect this quiet, sensitive student. There had been some problems encountered in his class scheduling. The biology teacher sent him to the principal's office when Tad refused to dissect a frog in a laboratory exercise. The principal, a very sensitive and caring person himself, excused Tad from the assignment.

Tad flourished in the classes he had taken in the area of fine arts. His poetry had been published in the school paper and won recognition at the state level. Many of his paintings adorned the hallways of the high school. Most of his paintings were of wildlife. A picture of a black stallion he had painted hung in the principal's office.

Tad studied the easel in front of him. On the canvas, a figure had been sketched in pencil. It resembled the face in a photograph laying on the desk next to him. The rough sketch gave few details, only suggesting the features to follow. It appeared that the face would be angelic, soft, and ovoid, with an alluring smile.

"Can I ever paint her as beautiful as she really is?" he wondered, looking at the photograph on the desk. Emma was Tad's closest friend. She was the only person he had ever shared his innermost feelings with.

The first year of high school had been very difficult for Tad. He had no friends. The boys in his class labeled him a sissy and he had bore the brunt of many jokes and persistent teasing. He was so bashful and timid that the girls in his class thought of him as a weirdo. He endured the teasing without any resentment, merely accepting it as part of life. He studied hard and made it a point never to offend anyone. Slowly the teasing abated. His excellence in the classroom soon became evident to his classmates. Many of them began to ask him for help in doing class assignments during the study hall period. Some of the girls even began to find him "cute" and flirted with him in the hallways as they changed classes.

He met Emma as he was walking to school the first morning of his junior year in high school. She was sitting on the curb at the side of the road, sobbing. Curious, he approached her. When he came near her side, she raised her head. It was then that he saw the kitten in her lap. There was blood matted in its fur and one of its front legs laid at an unusual angle to its body.

"What happened?" he asked.

"A car ran over my Tabby and didn't even stop," she choked between sobs.

"Is she hurt bad?"

"I don't know."

"Let's take her back to my house," he said, as he gently lifted the small animal from her lap.

With Emma closely following at his heels, they made their way back to his room in the basement of his grandfather's house. Once there, he placed the kitten in a box lined with an old bath towel. He then fashioned a crude splint for its broken front leg.

"I think she will be okay," he said. "We had better hurry or we'll be late for class." That afternoon, after classes were out, they ran back to Tad's house. They heard Tabby's hungry meow as they opened the basement door.

They had walked to and from school together almost every day since the morning that Tabby had been injured. Her parents had just moved to Laynard. Being an only child, born to parents late in life, she led a sheltered life. She attended a private junior high school for two years. Then her father retired and was unable to afford private schooling for her. Not wanting to send her to a large city school, they moved to Laynard, where she could finish high school in a small country environment.

Emma and Tad became inseparable. They shared all their dreams and hopes with each other. They talked about going to college. She wanted to be a nurse so she could help ease the pain and suffering of others. He hoped to be able to attend St. Ambrose College and enroll in the art program. In his dreams, his paintings brought happiness and joy to people, making them laugh, and bringing peace to those with troubled hearts.

There was one corner of his heart that Tad could not share with Emma. At times, when they were sitting close together on the sofa doing homework or when their bodies would accidentally touch as they walked to school together, a desire would spring up inside him that went beyond the feeling of friendship. It frightened him and he tried to repress it. He was afraid to tell her about it, afraid it would ruin their friendship.

Unable to get the flow of feeling he needed to make the painting come to life, Tad sat the easel in the store room behind the furnace. He didn't want anyone to see it until it was finished. He might decide never to show it to anyone, keeping it a secret just for himself.

Even though it was getting late, he decided to make an entry in his journal. He had kept a diary for as long as he could remember. It contained a composite of all the happiness, sorrows, fears, and dreams of his short life.

In a neat, flowing script he wrote: "Today was a happy day for me, as most days are now. I started a sketch of Emma. I will wait to start the painting until I decide how to combine her physical features with her spirit. I hope I can capture both. I received a letter from St. Ambrose College today. I have been accepted next year in their art school. I haven't told anyone yet. I'll tell Emma tomorrow on our way to school. I must also tell Mr. Haun, my counselor. He was the one that encouraged me to apply."

"That's wonderful!" exclaimed Emma when he told her the news the next morning. She flung her arms around his neck and kissed him on the lips. "You will be a famous artist some day."

Her reaction stunned him. They had never kissed before.

Explosive sensations like static electricity welled up inside him, almost taking his breath away.

"I will miss walking to school with you every day," he said.

"Don't worry, you'll make a lot of new friends at college," she said. They walked to school the rest of the way in silence.

Mr. Haun sensed the pride in Tad's voice when he handed him the official-looking envelope, saying, "I've been accepted."

"I was sure you would be. What did your parents say?"

Tad bowed his head. "I haven't told them yet. I never even told them that I was applying."

"Why not?" questioned Mr. Haun.

"I didn't think my father would be happy knowing that I wanted to be an artist, and my mother has so much on her mind taking care of my grandfather that I didn't want to bother her."

"Are they going to help you financially? The tuition at St. Ambrose is pretty expensive; then you've got books to purchase and living expenses on top of that."

All along Tad knew that he would have to ask someone to help him financially if he enrolled in college. He didn't think his father and Rosie were very well off, especially to loan him the amount of money he needed for four years of college. His mother was totally dependent on his grandfather, who only allowed her enough money to meet the bare essentials. This left his grandfather. Tad knew that his grandfather was extremely wealthy, although he didn't know just how well off he was. He owned numerous acres of rich bottom land west of Laynard near the river. He also owned a meat packing plant in the adjoining state. Tad knew that his grandfather could afford to help him with his college expenses, but hesitated asking him, fearing his refusal.

He had asked him for money once before, to pay for his class ring. His grandfather had ranted and raved, saying, "The only reason a person would wear a fancy ring like that would be to show off and flaunt his wealth." Tad was the only one of his classmates who didn't have a class ring.

"Good morning, Grandfather." Tad had decided that his grandfather was the only person he could turn to for financial help.

The old man had been bedridden for almost as long as Tad could remember. No one knew what his problem was, not even the family doctor. He had just refused to get out of bed one day and had spent the rest of his life lying in the big four-poster bed in a musty, dark room at the rear of the house.

In his younger days, the old man had been a very successful businessman. He made his fortune in farm land. The value he placed on a penny was well known in the community. When his name came up in conversation, it was often said that he had framed the first nickel he ever made, and that it hung under his portrait in the den of his house.

The old man had not liked the young man that came to court his daughter Amanda. He had been furious when she told him she was pregnant and wanted to marry that scoundrel. Letting them live in the basement of his house had been selfishly motivated. He wanted to keep control over them. He was actually happy when Joe left. "Good riddance!" he told the town folk. "My daughter can do better than that." Actually, he wanted to keep his daughter for his own welfare. He was afraid of growing old and having no one to take care of him.

Tad's mother had taken care of the old man all these years. She waited on him hand and foot, answering his every whim. He complained about the food she fixed him and cursed her when she was late bringing the paper to him in the morning. He berated her about the man to whom she had given her virginity, which had resulted in a bastard son. She tolerated his verbal abuse and meekly went about running the household. Tad heard her crying many nights in her bedroom.

The old man, propped up on two pillows, reading the morning newspaper, refused to acknowledge Tad's greeting.

"Could I talk to you about something important?" Tad asked in a pleading voice.

"Can't you see I'm busy reading the newspaper?"

"It won't take but a minute."

"Well, what do you want?" sighed the old man, folding the newspaper and laying it on top of the bedspread.

"I've been accepted to St. Ambrose college next year."

"So?"

"Would you help pay for some of the expenses? I would get a part-time job, but I couldn't make enough to pay for all the cost."

"Hell, no!"

"Maybe you could loan me the money and I could pay you back later," Tad begged.

The old man glared at Tad. "You really have the gall coming in here and asking me for money. All these years I've supported you and your mother because your worthless father wouldn't honor his responsibilities. You would have been in the poorhouse if it hadn't been for me. Not once did you ever thank me. Not once did you ever offer to pay me back or lift a finger to help support yourself. Instead, you've wasted your time and money sitting in your room painting worthless pictures. I know, I ask your mother where you are, you never come to see me. That and spending time horsing around with that young lady. You will probably knock her up and we'll have another bastard in the family. You're as worthless as your father. It's true, bad blood breeds bad blood."

Tad turned and fled from his grandfather's bedroom. He raced down the basement stairs, desperate for the familiarity of his own room with the animal paintings on the walls. A helpless feeling fell over him as he lay sobbing on his bed. Was his grandfather right? Were he and his father misfits in the world?

The next morning, Tad's mother thought it unusual that he was late for breakfast. When she opened the basement door to call him, she saw the lifeless legs dangling about two feet from the floor. Nearby was an overturned chair. In the center of the room was an easel, and on the canvas was a painting of an angel.

Sixteen

The limbs on the pine trees hung heavy with frost. A stiff north wind showed no mercy to a pair of chickadees attempting to keep their balance on the perch of a bird feeder hanging on a tree by the patio. The moisture in Joe's breath crystallized as he exhaled, forming small, dense clouds that drifted upward in the crisp air. The metallic knob on the mailbox bit at his fingers as he opened the lid and took out the morning paper. A chill penetrated his body and burst into a shiver. The wind chill must be near ten degrees below zero, he thought, as he turned his back to the wind. It would be a nice day to stay inside.

Rosie heard the front door open and felt the cold draft of air that accompanied it. She snuggled deeper under the wool blanket that covered the bed. There was a glow of satisfaction on her face. They had made love last night. It was the first time since Joe had been at the state hospital. It had not involved any of the extensive foreplay or exotic sexual passion which she was accustomed to, but she had enjoyed it immensely. After they were finished, Joe had held her closely.

The aroma of fresh-brewing coffee, acting as a mental alarm, awakened her. Pulling on her housecoat, she took a cigarette from the pack on the table beside the bed. The yellow flame of the cigarette lighter cast a ghostly pallor on her face as she inhaled deeply. Her coughing started immediately.

Joe had gone to his second follow-up examination at the state hospital the week before. At Rosie's insistence, Dr. McCall decreased the dose of lithium that Joe was taking. She complained about how tired Joe was all the time and how slow his actions were. She was sure the medication was responsible.

"The decrease in the dosage of medication should alleviate some of the side effects, but not totally eliminate them," Dr. McCall told her. "It may also result in a return of his previous symptoms. If they do return, they could be much more severe than they were before."

Rosie was sure she could tell a difference in Joe in just four days on the lower dosage of medication. He was beginning to get that spring back in his walk and his speech wasn't as slurred. Rosie was confident that Joe was on his way to full recovery and would regain that spirited, macho personality she had fallen in love with.

The phone rang and Rosie picked it up. "Could I speak with Joe?" the voice on the other end of the line asked. At first Rosie thought it was the same person that had called several times before asking for Joe, saying her name was Louise and that she was a client of his. Joe had become very upset by the calls, never answering them and telling Rosie that if the lady wanted to talk to him she should call the office.

"I'm sorry, he isn't here right now. Could I ask who's calling?"

"This is Tad's mother. Has he gone to work?"

"Oh, I didn't know that it was you. He's just outside starting the car. I'll get him." Strange, thought Rosie. She had never called their house before.

Rosie watched Joe as he listened to the voice on the other end of the line. She could feel the intense pain reflected on his face. "Thanks for calling," Joe said, his voice breaking. "I'll help you with the arrangements."

"What's wrong?" cried Rosie, as Joe began to tremble and fell to his knees on the kitchen floor.

"Tad hung himself last night."

From the deep abyss of Joe's subconscious mind came the visual images which he had buried in the past. They marched boldly into his conscious mind. He saw the body of the young boy laying in a pool of blood along the side of the road. He saw his own hands covered with blood, and he tried to wipe it off, but it merely spread and began to cover his whole body, suffocating him.

God was punishing him. He had taken the life of a young boy and now God had taken his son. He was responsible. He was the guilty one. "No sin goes unnoticed...the judgment of God will come in the final days and his punishment shall be just." He had heard a minister say that from the pulpit one Sunday morning. He was guilty. He was guilty. The words echoed in his brain.

Walls came crashing down around him. Snakes of fire licked at his body. Demons screamed in his ears. The black spider cautiously opened the door and stepped through the threshold. Its spindle-like legs, moving methodically, carried it into the conscious realm. It spun a magnificent web, sinister yet pure in geometric form. A nemesis for its final prey. Joe screamed and then lapsed into mental paralysis.

Mary's heart had leapt with joy when Gene came running in the back door of her sister's house in Morgan Creek. He was jumping up and down, crying, "Daddy's here!" She saw Al wearing a white shirt with the cuffs rolled up and the top button open, revealing the hair on his chest. He looked just like he had that first time she had seen him at the country dance years ago. There was still that mischievous look in his eyes and a hint of the cocky stance.

"I've come to take you home, Mary," he said tenderly, "if you'll give me another chance."

She answered him by burying her head in his chest and embracing him tightly.

Later, as the sun's rays warmed the crisp, late February air, they stood in silence, one on either side of the two adjacent grave markers, each pondering the power of death. "We must let them go now," Mary said, "knowing they are at peace."

"It took me a long time to realize that," said Al. "I just didn't want to let them go, especially Roy Lee. It almost destroyed me. I hope that God never forces me to face that kind of test again."

On their way home from the cemetery where Helen and Roy Lee were buried, Al reached across the seat and took Mary's hand. "I've been saving a surprise for you," he said. "You know the Anderson farm on the highway north of where we live? Well, I've been talking to Mr. Anderson, and he wants to quit farming and move into town. He offered to let me farm the land on a share-crop basis, with the option of eventually buying the farm."

"You mean we would be able to live in the farmhouse that's on the farm?" she asked excitedly.

"Sure; that's if you'd be willing to move. I told Mr. Anderson that I wanted to be sure it was okay with you before I signed an agreement."

Living in the Andersons' farmhouse went far beyond any of Mary's wildest dreams. She had been in the house a couple of times for quilting bees. It was a large, two-story colonial house with indoor plumbing and electricity, neither of which their present house had.

"I thought we could drive up there now and you could look

around the house," Al said. "And I want to talk to Mr. Anderson about how soon we should start spring plowing."

The Andersons' house was on a slight elevation of the otherwise flat 280 acres that made up one of the most productive farms in the county. The short driveway, which led to highway 65, was lined with neatly trimmed hedges. The house and all the outbuildings were painted white with green trim. A large orchard, with its leafless trees ready to bud forth in the spring, adorned the northwest corner of the farmstead.

"Hello, my dear, it's so nice to see you, Mary." Nola Anderson was of slight build with snow-white hair. It was an easy mistake to consider her fragile with a cursory look. On close examination, one was aware of the sinewy quality of her physique and the lines of determination in her face. She had worked side by side with her husband in the fields. Some of the neighbors even said that she could plow a straighter furrow with a five-span team of mules than her husband could.

The inside of the house was immaculate. Light danced on the highly polished hardwood floors. The furnishings were modest but elegantly decorated. A fine lace tablecloth adorned the oak table in the kitchen. A braided rug warmed the floor by the sofa in the living room.

"Carl's in the basement working on some antique furniture we picked up at a farm auction last week. I'll go fetch him," said Mrs. Anderson. "He'll be happy to see you."

The Andersons had married young. She had been sixteen and he seventeen. They were both the only children in their families and had been born late in the lives of their parents. Both their parents migrated from England, where they had been farmers. They had each bought parcels of rough farm land which lay side by side, separated by a small creek. They worked hard to clear the land of tree stumps and large boulders. They struggled to eke out a living, but always put more back into the land than they took out. By the time Carl and Nola took over the operation of the two farms, it was a highly productive 280-acre spread.

Nola became pregnant during the first year of their marriage.

The baby was stillborn at seven months. Whether it was the strenuous work she had been doing or a quirk of nature, the doctor didn't know. She was unable to get pregnant again, unable to produce any heirs for the land. As time went by, the Andersons prospered as a result of their hard work and respect for the land. When time began to take its toll, they were unable to put in the long hours necessary to operate a farm of that size. With troubled hearts, they worried about what would happen to the farm that had been part of their lives for so many years. They had no family, no one that appreciated the time and love that went into nurturing every inch of ground on their farm.

Carl became aware of the comments made by his neighbors about the young farmer that was renting land up near the bluffs. He was highly respected and made a profit from the less than fertile land which he farmed. Carl had been so impressed by what he heard that he made a point to become acquainted with Al. He had been extremely pleased with the knowledge of farming the young man seemed to have. He decided that here was a man that felt the same way about farming as he did. Here was someone that would appreciate and take care of his land.

Carl and Al had exchanged firm handshakes. Al was startled at the strength in the older man's grip.

"Let's sit at the kitchen table," Nola suggested. "I've just brewed a fresh pot of coffee." A large plate of chocolate chip cookies disappeared as they chatted.

"Well, what did Mary think of the prospect of moving in here and taking over the farming operation?" Carl asked Al.

"I think she thought it was too good to be true," answered Al, smiling at his wife.

"That's good," said Carl. "A happy wife makes things a whole lot easier for a man. When can you move in? Nola and I want to move into town right away and start fixing up the house we've purchased."

"I can move tomorrow," Mary joked.

"Let's plan on a week from this Saturday if the weather's okay," suggested Al.

* * *

Dr. McCall entered the hospital room, accompanied by his four psychiatric residents. "This is Joe," he said, opening the hospital file. "I first saw Joe approximately seven months ago when he was committed by his wife, on recommendation by his local physician, to state hospital for psychiatric evaluation. The initial diagnosis was manic-depression with an overriding guilt complex. Routine analysis under hypnosis did not uncover any past traumatic events that appeared responsible for his psychic state. His chief complaint at the time of admission was recurrent nightmares, which if I remember correctly, involved a spider.

"Initially the patient was placed on lithium and thorazine and the blood serum levels were checked every thirty days. The patient was apparently doing well, according to his wife's comments at the evaluation sessions.

"The patient was admitted last night through the emergency room. He had been transported by ambulance from Carville at the request of his local physician. On arrival, the patient was in a catatonic state. All of his vital signs were normal, but he was unresponsive to verbal stimuli."

The figure in the hospital bed lay in a semifetal position. His eyes were opened wide, unblinking, with constricted pupils. The only indication of life was the slight rising and falling of his chest.

Turning to the young female resident standing at his side, Dr. McCall said, "Dr. Monroe, what's your preliminary diagnosis of this patient?"

"Could it be catatonic schizophrenia?"

"I'm asking you," Dr. McCall said impatiently.

"Well, I would like to have some more information."

"Such as?"

"I'd like to know if there was something that happened to the patient that caused this reaction."

"Very good," said Dr. McCall sarcastically. "You do have some brain cells working. The patient's eighteen-year-old son committed suicide the night before last."

"That would support the diagnosis of catatonic schizophrenia," said Dr. Monroe, "but does that mean a mistake was made in the original diagnosis?"

"Not necessarily; more than one condition can exist at any given time."

"What treatment are you going to recommend?" asked Dr. McCall, addressing the resident standing on the other side of the hospital bed.

Dr. Bell, who had been taking copious notes, paused and thought for a moment. "I don't think I would recommend any treatment right now. I would wait a few days to see if the patient responds on his own."

"What if he doesn't come out of the catatonic state?"

"Electroshock treatments?"

"Correct," said Dr. McCall, closing the hospital record. As Dr. McCall left the room, the residents followed in single file like ducklings behind the mother duck.

Three female figures huddled together in the cemetery. A lonesome north wind penetrated their bodies. Workmen had to use picks to dig through the layer of frozen ground to prepare the grave. Large clods of sod, covered with glistening ice crystals, were piled at the side of the open pit. The only other person at the grave site was standing next to the casket. He was gently rocking from side to side, trying to repel the numbness creeping into his feet from the cold ground. The heavy black topcoat was buttoned tightly around his neck. The thick mittens made it difficult for him to turn the pages of the ancient Bible he held in his hands. "The Lord is my shepherd, I shall not want. He maketh me to lie down in green pastures. He leadeth me beside the still waters..."

It was a private funeral. Tad's mother had wanted it that way. She was aware of the stigma attached to the act of suicide and would have felt very self-conscious if anyone outside the family were present at the funeral service.

Rosie had loved Tad as much as a stepmother could. She drove all the way from the state hospital to pay respect to her husband's only son. Sadness gripped her heart that Joe could not be there. She knew Joe loved his son and in his own special way had attempted to be a good father.

The other person witnessing the burial was Emma, the girl with the angelic face. It was a face usually filled with happiness. Today it was a mask of sorrow streaked with tears. Gone was her friend with whom she had shared her fears, her sorrows, her love of life.

"...and now we commit the body of our beloved son to your care. He was with us such a short time but his love and kindness will remain in our hearts forever. We pray for his quick passage into your loving arms."

Emma placed a single red rose on the casket.

The old man tried to ignore the deep ache in his heart. His only grandchild had died an unnatural death. His seed had been destroyed. His essence would not be carried forward into future generations to immortalize him. It was his son-in-law's fault. Bad blood caused the seed to wither and die before it matured and bore fruit. "Curses be on that son of Satan!" the old man screamed to the empty walls. "May he suffer in hell the rest of his days for the grief he has caused me!"

Seventeen

"It's difficult to explain," said Dr. McCall, "but visualize the brain as a large switchboard sitting at the base of your brain. It sorts out the incoming messages and sends them to the proper area in the brain. There are literally hundreds of these messages coming through the switchboard every minute. They contain information about things we see, smell, taste, hear, and feel. If the messages are sent to the proper areas in the brain, there is a logical response to the information received. So, if the message of a hot stove is routed to the proper area in the brain, the brain sends out a message not to touch the stove. If the message is sent to the wrong area of the brain, there may be an abnormal response and one may actually touch the hot stove, or there may be no response at all. With Joe, the messages are being scrambled into the switchboard and are being transmitted to the wrong areas of the brain."

"Can he hear me when I talk to him?" Rosie asked.

"Yes, he can hear you, but he can't respond. It's as if his body is paralyzed."

"I think I understand," said Rosie. "What causes this to happen?"

"There are a variety of things. It could be a defense mechanism where the patient is afraid of the messages coming in, or messages that have come in during the past are too painful to cope with. Joe could have had a traumatic experience in the past which has caused a malfunction in the switchboard."

"Dr. McCall said you can probably hear me," Rosie said to the expressionless face in the hospital bed. Glucose dripped through IV tubing into the vein on the back of Joe's hand. "I wanted to tell you how much I love you and how much I miss having you at home. He told me that there was probably some horrible experience you had some time in the past that is causing you to be sick. He said you have buried it in your mind and refuse to deal with it. I want you to know that whatever it was, I will understand and will try to help you any way I can." Rosie was sure she saw a flicker of acknowledgment in his eyes.

Chief resident Monroe swore lightly under her breath as the hot coffee burned the roof of her mouth. She hurriedly thumbed through a hospital record, making notes in a small spiral notebook.

"I take it the day isn't starting off like you had hoped," said Dr. Bell as he pulled up a chair beside her.

The hospital lounge was filled with residents. You could tell the ones that were finishing their shifts. They were leisurely sipping their coffee as they wrote up patient records. Those just coming on board were shoving fresh doughnuts in their mouths and taking quick sips of coffee. Closely watching the clock, they would dash off to their assigned wards at the last minute.

"I forgot that we have grand rounds tomorrow at six A.M." Dr. Monroe replied. "Dr. McCall assigned me to present Joe, the patient in room 237, as the first case. Nobody seems to be able to make a diagnosis on the patient. He's been in that catatonic state now for over a week. He may never come out of it. What a way to spend the rest of your life."

"Has Dr. McCall given any more thought to using shock treatments?"

"He hasn't mentioned it to me, but I think I'll take a chance and recommend it at rounds tomorrow. Hope McCall doesn't bite my head off."

"I not only recommend it, but I feel it's the only choice we have." said Dr. McCall. "We discussed it at rounds this morning and we are in agreement that electroshock treatments should begin immediately."

Rosie shuddered. She had heard so many horror stories about shock treatments. "How can they help him?" she asked.

"Well, remember the malfunctioning switchboard in the brain we talked about the other day? Shocking the system may restore the circuits in the switchboard, allowing it to function properly."

"Will he feel much pain?"

"The procedure involves the administration of a series of three to four exposures to a voltage of electricity similar to that in an outlet in your house. To answer your question, he may feel some discomfort at the time, but most patients don't remember it."

Reluctantly, Rosie signed her name on the treatment release form. She hoped she was doing what Joe would have wanted her to do. "When will you begin treatment?"

"Tomorrow morning at 7:00 A.M."

The hospital orderly checked the work orders for the

patient in room 237: Prep for electroshock treatments—patient scheduled in O.R. at 7:00 A.M. "So, they're going to fry another one," the orderly thought, as he switched on the bright overhead light in room 237. The patient was lying curled up on his side with eyes wide open. "Good morning," said the orderly. Must be a real loony, he thought when the patient made no response.

The orderly lathered both left and right temples with soap. Then with a safety razor he shaved off the hair in front of Joe's ears. He exposed two square inches of white skin in each temple region. He then shaved Joe's lower legs and ankles. He had to rinse the razor often because of the abundance of long black hair on Joe's legs. "There, you're all set to be wired," said the orderly.

One wheel on the gurney refused to track with its three companions. It wobbled and squeaked as nurse Maria maneuvered it down the sterile corridor with the bare green painted walls. When they reached the operating room, Joe was transferred to a stationary bed surrounded with numerous monitoring devices. Arm boards were swung out from underneath the bed. The operating room nurses secured Joe's arms with the leather cuffs attached to the arm boards. A laboratory technician securely attached cathodes to the clean-shaven spots in front of Joe's ears. Metal cuffs attached to his ankles completed the circuit.

"Don't forget the mouth prop," instructed Dr. McCall. "We don't want him biting his tongue off."

A nurse quickly placed the hard latex rubber appliance in Joe's mouth and secured it with clamps under his lower jaw.

"Everyone clear of the table?" Dr. McCall asked from his position behind the control panel. The laboratory technician answered by giving the thumbs up sign.

Dr. McCall pressed the contact button on the control panel. The charged atoms of electricity surged through the body on the table, ricocheting off bone and tearing at muscles. The body arched and appeared to levitate above the surface of the bed as the muscles shortened and went into spasm.

Clinching jaws caused the teeth to bite deeply into the rubber mouth prop. A moan emanated from the patient's throat. A wet spot appeared on the sheet where he had soiled himself.

An aura of colors exploded in the hemispheres of his brain, blinding him to all sensation. The black spider was startled by the intrusion of an unknown force—a force more evil than itself. The force destroyed the web that had encased Joe's mental processes for the past few weeks. The spider retreated into the dark depths of the subconscious to await another time for its prey to weaken.

Joe stared at the creature on the window sill. What was it? His mind searched for a word. Deep within his memory bank lay the answer. Suddenly the mental computer crackled and the bold letters ROBIN appeared on the screen. Sure, it is a robin, a bird, how could he have forgotten? Other words flooded into his thoughts: The early bird gets the worm. Why did those words appear? Were they juxtaposed in his memory?

"I'm hungry," said Joe as nurse Maria hung another liter of glucose solution on the pole attached to the side of the hospital bed.

She turned to him and smiled. "Welcome back, you've been gone quite a long time."

"Where am I?" he asked, looking around the hospital room, trying to put into perspective what he saw.

"You're on the psychiatric ward at state hospital," Maria said. "You've been here almost two weeks."

"Why can't he go home?" asked Rosie. "He's not in a coma anymore. He seems all right to me."

"Granted, he's come out of the catatonic state," replied Dr. McCall, "but we still aren't sure why he originally went into it. He could very easily relapse anytime. I want to keep him here under observation for six to eight weeks. Believe me, if I thought it was safe to send him home, I'd check him out today."

* * *

It was a beautiful day to move. Al and Mary had been ready to move two weeks before, but an early spring snowstorm had thwarted their plans. Mr. Anderson offered his tractor with a wide-boxed wagon to move their possessions. Al had never driven a tractor before. He was like a boy with a new toy.

"Appears to me you're having too much fun with that thing," said Mary as Al jerked the tractor to a stop in front of the back porch.

"It'll never replace my mules," Al said jokingly. "It doesn't know the difference between 'gee' and 'haw.'"

Mary packed all of the small items and labeled the boxes to facilitate unpacking. One box was simply labeled "memories." It contained a variety of items. In a small black velvet box was a Medal for Excellence with Roy Lee's name inscribed on the back. He won it at the county spelling bee when he was in the third grade. There was a miniature lace bonnet that Helen had worn the Sunday morning she was baptized. Of special value were two aging photographs of people from an earlier age. They were pictures of each set of her grandparents on their wedding day. They had all died before she was born. It was the only physical evidence of her heritage that she possessed. She looked at the pictures often, staring into the eyes, trying to communicate with them. In daydreams she talked with them and told them that she was their granddaughter and that she loved them very much.

Also in the box was a small harmonica. It belonged to John, her older brother. When she was a baby, John would sit by her crib and play songs for her. Even though she had been quite young at the time, she could still remember some of the songs and hear the sounds of the notes made by the old harmonica. John died from tuberculosis when he was sixteen years old. She was five years old at the time. For many nights during the following years, she slept with the harmonica under her pillow. In her dreams she could still hear the music.

In the bottom of the box was a cigar box with a sturdy rubber band around it. Inside were hundreds of Indian head pennies and numerous other coins minted before the turn of the century. The coins had been entrusted to Mary by Al's father at the time of their marriage with the instructions that they be given to their oldest child at the age of eighteen.

"You want to check the house once more to be sure you haven't forgotten anything?" asked Al as he secured the last cardboard box on the loaded wagon.

"Did the back door always squeak like that?" wondered Mary as she entered the house. Her footsteps echoed in the stark nakedness of the rooms. A wave of nostalgia swept over her. She had been so excited to move into the Anderson's house, but now doubts surfaced in her mind. Suddenly the emptiness was filled with memories.

This old farmhouse had been their first home. Only the walls knew some of their most intimate secrets. Where there had once been laughter and crying, only silence reigned. The solid plank floors bore witness to the hardships they endured. All of their children had been born here. It had been a haven, a refuge for them as they struggled through the lean years of life.

Mary knelt at the top of the stairs. "Thank you, dear Lord, for this old house and the many blessings it has given to my family."

Al led the way down the driveway with the tractor pulling the wagon stacked high with their possessions. Mary followed in the car with Gene, Jimmy and Shirley in the back seat amid boxes of dishes and glasses wrapped in old newspapers. They turned north on highway 65 at the country schoolhouse. When the Anderson's house came into view, Mary's nostalgic mood quickly disappeared.

Eighteen

Dr. Macke slipped into his white starched laboratory-style jacket. The aroma from the freshly poured cup of coffee on his desk teased his senses of taste, smell, and sight. He gently blew on the surface of the liquid, cooling the portion nearest the rim. The hot coffee threatened to burn his tongue but cooled as he swallowed it. "It couldn't act that fast," he thought as a surge of well-being filled his body. "It must be psychosomatic."

Laying on his desk, neatly typed, was a schedule of his patients for the day. Ever since he started practice twenty years ago, he always made it a practice to get to the office each morning in time to have a cup of coffee and review the records of the patients he would see that day. He noted any little personal details he had written, such as the name of a pet belonging to a pediatric patient. Patient's birthdays were underlined in red, as were anniversaries and graduation dates. On some records he indicated whether the patient seemed more comfortable being called by their first name or by "Mr." or "Mrs." On a limited number of records was written, "Pecan." This was a code word for patients who were habitual complainers, that always felt something was wrong and usually made up their own diagnosis before they came to see him.

Knowing the personalities and traits of the people he treated gave him an advantage in understanding the make-up of the individual patient and aided him in diagnosing their illnesses.

During his years of practice he had become convinced that a large percent of the everyday illness he saw could be cured merely by establishing proper patient-doctor relationships. He referred to it as chairside manner when he was asked to lecture at the county medical meetings. Lending a sympathetic ear, showing respect and concern, placing a hand gently on a patient's shoulder, all were an important part of his armament in the treatment of his patients. He was convinced that this approach was the reason he enjoyed the largest medical practice in the county.

At the top of the schedule, squeezed in at 8:15, and written in pencil, was "Rosie: emergency."

"Must be something serious," he mused. The receptionist had been instructed to only schedule emergencies at 11:30 A.M. or 4:30 P.M.

Rosie was surprised to find a parking spot directly in front of the building where Dr. Macke's office was located. Usually the lot was filled and one had to park at a metered space on the adjacent side streets. The building was a modern medical complex serving a four-county area. It was well equipped and housed many of the medical subspecialties found usually only in the big city hospitals.

As she turned off the ignition, she looked at her reflection in the rearview mirror. The dark rings around her eyes and the swollen tissue directly below them reflected the lack of sleep from the night before. The furrowed brow was in response to her inner turmoil of concern.

The night before, enjoying a glass of wine and a cigarette, she had been watching the evening news when she had one of her recurrent coughing spells. At first she wasn't concerned, she had had them before. They were usually nonproductive and only lasted two or three minutes. This one became so severe that she was gasping between coughs to get enough oxygen to her lungs.

Suddenly a warm, salty taste filled her mouth. She ran to the bathroom and spit in the sink. Saliva streaked with bright red blood ran down the side of the sink and disappeared into the drain. Terror gripped her. What was happening to her body? She had had coughing seizures for years but had never coughed up blood before.

Rosie's chest radiographs were still wet with fixer solution as Dr. Macke hung them up on the bright view box. The radiologist down the hall would evaluate them later, but he wanted to take a preliminary look at them. Even his eyes, uneducated at reading radiographs, immediately recognized the small nodular images in both the left and right lung area. It undoubtedly was small cell carcinoma of the lung. It was probably in an advanced stage considering the number of lesions in both lungs. More tests would have to be done before a definite diagnosis could be made. There was little doubt in Dr. Macke's mind.

Rosie's fingernails dug deeply into the palms of her hands. Dozens of questions surfaced in her frenzied mind. The one that materialized verbally was: "How much longer do I have to live?"

Dr. Macke had anticipated the question; in fact, it was the first question almost every patient asked when first told that they had cancer. The question placed him in a very difficult and delicate position. It placed him in a dilemma. He proposed to his colleagues that honesty with a patient was always the best policy. He could tell Rosie that the five-year survival rate of patients diagnosed with small cell carcinoma of the lung was less than four percent. He could tell her that statistically she had less than six months to live. This response would probably wipe out the one ingredient that might effect a cure. That ingredient was hope. He had to leave a ray of optimism for the patient to cling to, a chance, no matter how small, to sustain hope.

"Well, I don't want to sound too optimistic because it is a very malignant type of cancer, but with aggressive treatment we may be able to slow it down or maybe even get it into remission for a period of time. You could have months or maybe even years to live." He didn't mention anything about the quality of life she might have to endure.

"What kind of treatments will I need?"

"I'll have to refer you to a specialist at University Hospital. There's a relatively new specialty in the field of medicine called oncology which deals with the treatment of cancer. Dr. Keller, at University Hospital, is one of the pioneers of this specialty."

"I see in your record that we have Joe listed as the next of kin in case of an emergency. Since he's confined to the state hospital we should list someone else."

"There is no one else. I don't have any family living. Neither does Joe. We only have each other."

Dr. Macke fought off the sympathy that rose in his heart for this unfortunate lady. "I suggest we schedule you immediately with the oncologist so we can start treatment as soon as possible."

As Rosie got up to leave, Dr. Macke took her hand. "Don't you worry now, we'll give it our best shot."

She dropped the half-empty cigarette package in the trash receptacle outside Dr. Macke's office.

The name, Dr. Keller, in bold print, filled the upper panel of the heavy oak door. Below the name printed in smaller lettering was: "Specializing in Oncology." He was a wizened little man, almost elf-like in stature. To compensate for his size and appearance, he put on a very authoritative and arrogant facade for both his colleagues and patients.

Rosie sat on the edge of the examination table, clad only in a hospital gown. She chewed at the hangnail on the forefinger of her left hand. Doctors made her nervous and tense. She was intimidated by them. They were like gods that held the power of life and death over you. Her body jerked as the door to the examination room burst open.

The intruder announced in a shrill and triumphant tone of voice, "I am Dr. Keller. I will be in charge of prescribing and dispensing your treatment. I want you to know from the beginning what to expect from the treatment I recommend. You should buy yourself a wig because you'll lose all your hair. Also, you will have repeated bouts of nausea and vomiting. They will probably become very severe. Once we start, we cannot stop until the full course of treatment has been completed. So, if you have any question about whether or not you want to go through with treatment, now is the time to make that decision."

The stark abrasiveness of his words confused Rosie. What was he trying to tell her? "Do you recommend the treatment?" she asked.

"It's the accepted, standard procedure. You, however, have the choice of whether or not you want to try to extend your period of life."

Tears of fear filled her eyes as she nodded her head.

"Good. We'll start the radiation therapy on Monday."

The visit to Dr. Keller's office had physically drained her. The hope that Dr. Macke had planted was completely destroyed. She lay in bed, too weak to get up and too tired to sleep. She was only forty-four years old, too young to die. This should be the prime time of her life, a time of enjoying the fruits of a family and anticipation of grandchildren. All this had eluded her. As numbness shrouded her mind, thoughts of her childhood surfaced.

She was three years old when her mother died. No one knew why; the doctor said that she just lost her will to live. Her father, still a young man, found that a three-year-old child proved to be a burden to his social life. The numerous young ladies he courted didn't especially want the responsibility of taking care of someone else's three-year-old kid. Her childhood was spent being shuffled between aunts and uncles and grandparents. They all extracted the wages for her care. By the time she was twelve years old she was being sexually abused by six family members, five uncles and one aunt. In desperation, she had run away at the age of sixteen. Being mature beyond her age, she could pass as being in her twenties. Jumping from job to job, she finally settled in the town of Knox, about thirty miles north of Carville, with an older couple that befriended her.

Working as a waitress at a local café, she made many friends, and the kindness shown to her by the couple she lived with gave her life some stability. She had been there three years when one morning there was a knock on the door of her room. It was the owner of the house. "The missus died last night," he said. Two weeks later he promised her he'd give her anything she wanted if she would go to bed with him. He was fifty-six years old. She had consented, on one condition—that he marry her. Finally, she had found someone who cared for her, or so she thought. They were married for three years before he ran off with someone else.

The first time she laid her eyes on Joe, an impulse had surged throughout every sensory fiber in her body. His lithe muscular body triggered a physical desire that she had never experienced before. She decided that this was the man she wanted to marry.

Joe had been obsessed with her lovemaking, consumed by the physical excitement she stirred within him. His first wife complained every time he suggested they make love. Rosie became excited by the mere touch of his hands and never refused his advances.

As time went by, the sexual desires began to wane, but her love for him continued to grow and they had a comfortable relationship. She suspected that he was seeing other women, but never confronted him with the fact. She tolerated his frequent escapades, knowing that when they ended he would return to her bed. She felt guilty that she was unable to give him a child, which he wanted so badly. Early on she encouraged him to try to get custody of his son Tad. She had fallen in love with the young child Joe brought home on weekends when he had visitation rights. She would have been happy to raise him as her own child.

Joe had no family left since his son passed away. He never heard from his father after he had been released from jail when Joe was sixteen years old. She never heard from her father after she had left home. "He's probably dead by now," she thought. She hoped all her aunts and uncles had died and gone to hell. She still had dreams of being fondled as a child and forced to commit sexual favors if she wanted to be loved and have a place to live.

There was only Joe and her left. They needed each other now more than ever. What would happen to Joe if she wasn't there to take care of him?

Across the room, his roommate was confined to his bed in restraining wraps. He was forty-two years old and fantasized that he was a truck driver. He made guttural sounds imitating the shifting of gears as he drove his eighteen-wheeler down the four-lane highway. He's really a loony, thought Joe.

"Have you got it in high gear yet, Charley?" he chuckled. "If you haven't, you'll never make it to Kansas City on time."

"Not going to Kansas City. Got a load of steel, going to Pittsburgh. Bbbroon brom brruuuu…shit."

"What's wrong?"

"There's a weigh station up ahead and I'm overloaded."

Now that guy is crazy, thought Joe. If I stay around here much longer, I may end up as nuts as the rest of the people stuck in here.

"Time for your medicine," said nurse Maria as she handed him a paper cup containing numerous different colored tablets.

"I'm feeling fine. I don't need any of that stuff."

"I only do what the doctor tells me to do, and he says you need it, so be a good boy and don't give me any crap."

Joe visualized the plump figure hiding under the tight-fitting uniform. "If you really want to make me feel better, I've got a suggestion."

"Be careful, big boy. You're talking to a tiger that just might eat you up."

"You're my kind of broad," he grinned as he popped the pills in his mouth and reached for the tepid glass of water sitting on the bedside stand. "You'd think this place could afford ice for the drinking water."

The sedative slowly took command of his body, causing a false sense of sleepiness. His mind rebelled, continuing to evoke thoughts. Where was Rosie? He tried to think how long it had been since she had been there. It was at least three days. Was she abandoning him? He needed her, there was no one else. Who would take care of him? Slowly his thoughts melted into dreams as the medication penetrated his body.

The image looked familiar. He peered at it through the veil of dreams. It was his son Tad. As he drew near, there was a metamorphosis of the image. It became a young boy lying in a pool of blood. He turned to run. His extremities flayed at the web that entangled his body. Terror exploded like fireworks. He knew the creature was coming. He saw the door slowly opening. Long, black, hairy legs danced in space. A guttural scream of agony escaped his lips. An icy numbness intervened, canceling out the images. The door closed, leaving darkness. The intruder bided its time.

Nurse Maria was nodding in sleep at the nurse's station when she heard the scream. Quickly she ran to the end of the hall where the noise had come from. With a flashlight in her hand she scanned the room and the beam came to rest on Joe. His bed was in disarray. She gently straightened the sheets and covered Joe with a blanket. The bottom sheet was soaked with sweat.

Must have been a lulu of a nightmare, she thought. As she turned to leave she noted movement in the other bed. "Did he wake you?"

"Yes, I've been listening to him for ten minutes or more. I think he's crazy."

Nineteen

The hot summer heat penetrated the stone walls of the state hospital, overloading the antiquated cooling system. Large fans droned in the hallways, creating a false breeze. Rosie fanned herself with an old issue of *Newsweek* magazine. Swallowing, she tried to fight off the surge of nausea.

"Sorry to keep you waiting," said Dr. McCall as he entered the room. His secretary had called her the day before asking if she could meet with him today. "Joe's nightmares are returning. He's incoherent much of the time. In other words, I think his mental health is deteriorating. I recommend that we try additional treatments of electroshock therapy."

Sweat broke out on her forehead as she fought off another wave of nausea. "Do you think he will ever be well enough to go home?"

"I must tell you, I don't think the prognosis is too good. We still have a long way to go in understanding mental illness. The medications we have sometimes effect a cure in one patient, but not the next. In Joe's case, we haven't been too successful. Also, I should inform you that the board of directors is putting pressure on me. The usual length of time a patient is confined to the psychiatric ward is six to eight weeks before we transfer them to another facility. Even though Joe has been here going on three months, I've suggested that we keep him another couple of weeks so we can give him further treatment."

"What then?"

"If he doesn't respond, we would have to transfer him to the state mental care facilities, which is considered long-term care."

What little hope she had faded away. They were giving up on him. No one had used the term "mentally insane," but she knew. She had never been in the mental care center but had heard horrible stories about life inside its walls—patients tied in their beds, urinating on themselves, lying in their own waste. She had never heard of anyone leaving once they had been admitted.

They were heavily drugged, living the rest of their lives in limbo. Was this the life that awaited Joe? Why was he being punished? What had he done to deserve this? Had he committed some kind of terrible crime for which he had to pay? Was this justice? A silent sob stuck in her chest.

Four people took time out of the day to pay their respects to Rosie. Joe's boss, two neighbor ladies, and Joe's ex-wife Amanda stood facing the minister as he recited the virtues of death over life "...to live in one of the rooms Jesus has prepared for us, being a part of His eternal kingdom. Never again to feel pain or sorrow. Abiding in peace with God the Father."

Dying had not been kind to Rosie. Midway through her radiation treatment, large clumps of her red hair had fallen out. She purchased a wig, but it looked unnatural. She couldn't match the color of her natural hair. Near the end she merely wore a knit hat to hide her baldness.

She had watched the heavy chemical fluid dripping into the main line of the IV tube forming an oily mixture with the lactose solution before entering the vein in her arm. The tissue around the puncture sight was red and inflamed. She felt a burning sensation as the toxic material entered her veins. Once in her bloodstream, the chemical spread to all parts of her body, destroying both normal cells and cancer cells in its wake.

After the third chemotherapy treatment, she began to experience nausea accompanied with fits of vomiting. This worsened during the remainder of her treatments and extracted a heavy toll on her once supple body. Large folds of loose, sallow skin appeared as her weight dropped below one hundred pounds.

Her greatest fear was not that of dying, but of leaving Joe all alone with no one to take care of him. She visited him almost every day, except toward the end. She had not told him of her cancer, afraid of upsetting him. He seemed unaware of the change in her appearance. At times she even wondered if he recognized who she was. Most of the times when she visited him he would lie in his bed babbling about things like spiders and demons, and how we would all pay for the sins we committed.

The question of who would take care of Joe when she died plagued her for many weeks. Who would go visit him and be sure that he was treated properly? In desperation she had gone to see Amanda, Joe's ex-wife.

A haze of tears clouded Amanda's eyes as she stared at the barren casket. Why was the world so cruel? She had been surprised when Rosie appeared at her door a few weeks ago. She had only met her twice before. As they talked, sympathy flowed out of her heart for this desperate creature. During the following weeks, a strong bond formed between them. They talked about Tad and Joe and their own fate in life. She promised Rosie that she would visit Joe and look after him.

* * *

As Amanda opened the front door of her father's house, a booming voice rang out. "Where the hell have you been so long?"

She walked into the bedroom and looked at the figure lying in the bed. He's going to outlive all of us, she thought. "I've been to a funeral," she replied.

"Who died?"

"Joe's wife, Rosie."

"Why in the hell would you go to her funeral? The whore took your husband away from you by spreading her legs for him."

She grit her teeth in anger. How could one man be so evil? she wondered.

Early the next morning, after she fed the old man his breakfast, she slipped quietly out of the house. She didn't ask him if she could use the car, knowing he would refuse to let her have it to drive to the state mental care center.

Joe arched his neck as the buzzing sounds came closer. Finally he located the source. Two large green flies were circling high above his bed. He recognized them, they had been there the day before. They swooped down, coming dangerously close to his face. His hand moved in a delayed attempt to intercept them. One landed on the rim of his drinking glass and began gracefully grooming its front legs. He was fascinated by its delicate balance and rhythmic movements. Its eyes seemed magnified in comparison to the rest of its body. I wonder if it can see me, Joe thought.

Joe had been transferred from the state hospital to the state mental care center. No definite diagnosis accompanied the transfer letter. Dr. McCall merely stated that the patient was not able to care for himself due to mental deficiencies. Being classified as nonviolent, he was placed in a ward with ten other inmates. Joe carefully surveyed his surroundings. He had been fortunate. His bed was at the far end of his side of the ward. He could turn his back on all the activity of his wardmates and take consolation in the green blank wall adjacent to his bed. He noted the bars on the windows. Were they there to keep people in or people out? He tried but couldn't form an answer. He was glad the bars were there. They kept out the spider.

"Joe, you have someone to see you in the visitors' room," said Sadie, the stout female orderly that appeared at his bedside. "You get your robe on and I'll try to find the wheelchair."

Joe's heart quickened. "It must be Rosie," he thought. She hadn't forgotten about him. It had been over four weeks since she had been to see him.

Amanda sat nervously at one of the small tables in the visitor's room. The large room which also served as a patient's recreation area was empty except for two other visitors and two patients. It was easy to separate the visitors from the patients. The patients had on oversized gray robes which resembled large dyed gunnysacks.

She did not recognize Joe when Sadie parked his wheelchair on the opposite side of the table from her. His once well-groomed curly black hair was now peppered with gray and lay matted on his head. His eyes, with dilated pupils, peered out of sunken sockets.

"Joe?"

"Who are you?"

"I'm Amanda, remember me?"

"Where's Rosie?"

"She couldn't come. She sent me to see you."

"But I want to see Rosie."

Joe pulled back as Amanda reached for his hand. "She can't come to see you anymore."

"Why?"

"She died last week."

The scream lodged in his throat, choking him. He could make no sounds. He wanted to kick the floor and pound on the table, but his extremities made no movement. He could not release the pain. The world exploded around him.

That night Joe was confined to an isolation cell. With the

help of the security guard, Sadie was able to place the restraining cuffs around his wrists and ankles. His tortured screams echoed throughout the walls of the mental care center. Devils danced in the hallways. The black spider pranced defiantly forward from its unconscious abode. Its legs moved in unison as if in step to some ancient march.

Most of the other patients were quiet that night. Many of them sensed the agony of their fellow inmate. The deep innermost part of their souls asked, Why us?

Amanda did not answer the old man's questions when she returned home that evening. She tiptoed to her room and quietly closed the door behind her. Sobs were the only response to the ravings of the old man in the next room.

Twenty

Al smelled the electricity in the air as he watched the dark clouds gather on the horizon. Another rain, perfectly timed. He had just finished laying by his corn, and today they had gotten the third cutting of alfalfa hay put in the barn. There had only been two years during the fifteen years he had farmed the Anderson place that the weather had an undesirable effect on the crops. One year it had been so dry that the silk on the premature ears of corn didn't pollinate properly, resulting in stunted cobs, some of which contained no kernel formation, but merely laid barren under the shucks. Instead of letting the whole crop go to waste, which many of his neighbors had done, Al cut the immature plants while they were still green and chopped them into silage. He dug a large pit behind the barn and filled it with the silage, covering it with tarps to protect it from the elements. The next winter, when the price of grain skyrocketed, he used the silage as a supplement to fatten a herd of feeder cattle. The price of beef cattle had been high that year. He made a handsome profit.

Then there was the year when it rained all fall. Even fields that had adequate drainage tile became quagmires, preventing the timely harvesting of the crops. They had no choice except to wait for the ground to freeze. The crop was harvested in the dead of winter. Many days they had to knock the snow off the shucks before the ears of corn could be retrieved. Much of the corn was left in the fields and later plowed under in preparation for the next season.

The other thirteen years he raised bumper crops, and it appeared he would again this year. The land had been so productive that he calculated being able to pay the farm off the following year. All the hard work, the scrimping, the doing without many luxuries had been worth it. He had always dreamed of having a piece of land he could call his own.

A cowbell tinkled in the distance. Gene and Jimmy were directing the milking short-horns into the milking shed. The herd had increased to fifty-two animals. Nine of the older cows were fresh and had to be milked morning and night. Gene and Jimmy had the responsibility for the chores. This involved the tending of the chickens and hogs and the milking of the cows. Their allowance came from the cream they separated from the milk and the eggs they sold to the local produce store.

Al knelt down and picked up a handful of black soil. He gently crumbled it as it sifted through his fingers. He could feel its inherent richness. Who would till it after he was gone? he wondered. Mary had presented him with his third son, David, two years after they moved. He hoped one of the boys would stay and tend the farm. He would miss Gene, who was leaving in the fall to attend the university to study to become a teacher. Jimmy, even though he was only a sophomore in high school, wanted to get a job in town so he wouldn't have to do chores.

Maybe David will take a liking to the land and appreciate it as I have, Al thought.

With a paring knife in one hand and a potato in the other, Mary swirled her dress in a waltz step. The air was filled with the lyrical notes of the "Blue Danube Waltz," by Strauss. Shirley sat at the piano, her eyes fixed intently on the keyboard. At the age of fifteen she was already an accomplished pianist.

She had taken lessons from Nola Anderson. Every Tuesday evening, shortly after they had moved into the Andersons' house, Mary would invite the Andersons to join them in the evening meal. After the meal was finished, Mary would insist on doing the dishes by herself, leaving Nola free to work with Shirley on the piano. Al and Carl would retire to the family room with their hot coffee and exchange the weekly gossip of Laynard.

Nola refused to take any payments for her instruction. Mary, in return, supplied them with fresh eggs and vegetables from the garden. In the wintertime when it snowed, Al and Gene would clear the driveway of the small home the Andersons had bought in Laynard.

A deep friendship grew between the two families. The Andersons looked upon Al and Mary as the offspring they could never have. The children became their grandchildren and fulfilled a longing that had plagued their hearts for years.

Mary waited until Shirley had finished practicing for her lesson the next day and then announced that supper was ready. There was a scraping of chairs as the family gathered around the table.

With their hands joined around the table, Mary invoked God's blessing for the food before them. Steam arose from the array of bowls on the old oak table. Each spewed forth its own characteristic aroma. A clamorous atmosphere ensued as serving spoons scraped the bottom of dishes and empty glasses clinked for refills.

"I'm going to the cemetery tomorrow. Anyone want to go with me?" Mary asked. She made annual pilgrimages to visit the graves ever since Roy Lee died.

"Why don't we all go down early in the morning?" Al suggested.

She met his eyes with a smile of approval. There was a flicker of tenderness in his eyes as he silently said, I love you.

"How long ago did Roy Lee die?" asked Jimmy.

"Sixteen years ago tomorrow," his father answered.

"No wonder I can't remember him. I wasn't even two years old."

"You n-n-never did f-f-find out w-who did it, d-d-did you?" asked Gene. He always wondered what kind of evil individual it was that had taken his brother's life, never to have contacted the family to ask forgiveness for causing them so much grief. "I w-w-wonder if he is s-s-still living? I h-hope God m-m-made him suffer."

"Vengeance does not belong to us. It is not our place to judge," said Mary. "I forgave him a long time ago and even though I don't know who it was, I pray to God that his soul might be saved."

There was silence around the table as the significance of Mary's words filled their hearts, and they grew in wisdom and understanding.

Outside, large raindrops fell from the heavens. Exploding on contact, they penetrated the rich ground, satisfying the thirst of the young plants. The plants grew and produced.

Moe Hendersen luxuriated in the coolness of his office. The rain the night before had not relieved the hundred degree temperatures. In fact, it had increased the humidity, making it seem warmer than the thermometer indicated. Gone was the noisy floor fan which had attempted to keep his office bearable for so many years. One day it just made a belching sound and filled the room with the odor of burning rubber. Moe tried to repair it but to no avail. The city council recommended a window air conditioner, but he persisted in his request for a central air conditioning system. He was curious about the memo Louise left on his desk the afternoon before: "The president of the city council wants you to meet him at the Legion Club for lunch tomorrow. Be there by 12:30. (He sounded as if it was important.)"

What is it now? thought Moe. Was it a complaint about something he had done or another one of the council's harebrained ideas they wanted him to support?

He was surprised at the number of cars in the Legion Club's parking lot. "They must be having their sparerib special," he mused. "That's the only thing that could draw such a crowd."

Being an advocate of punctuality, he entered the front door of the Legion Club at exactly 12:30. He was stunned by the cheer that arose as he crossed the threshold. It took a few seconds for his eyes to adjust to the darkened room. As the room came into focus it appeared as if all the townspeople were crowded about the tables. A large banner hung from the ceiling: "Thanks for 20 years of service." Someone in the crowd started chanting, "For he's a jolly good fellow...," and the rest of the voices joined in.

He squeezed into the space reserved for him at the head table between his wife and Moe Junior. He never was one for self-acclaim, but this show of support and respect by the people of Laynard overwhelmed him. Different city dignitaries proposed toasts, many of them citing humorous or comical antecdotes about his activities during his tenure as chief of police.

The last to speak was the mayor of Laynard. His tone was serious. The crowd became silent. "Moe, in recognition of your twenty years of bringing law and order to the town of Laynard, I would like to present you with this plaque noting your high principles of justice in serving our community. We hope you will be with us for another twenty years. Now I think it's time to bring on the special for today." Turning to the proprietor that stood by the kitchen door, he said, "Bring on the spareribs."

Moe's wife, Moe Junior, and Louise were waiting for him in his office when he returned. He felt obligated to stay after the meal and chit-chat, shaking hands with those people who had entrusted him with keeping the peace in their town. His wife's eyes filled with tears of pride as she embraced him.

"Congratulations, sir," said Moe Junior, clasping his hand. "This has been a very special day for you. I hope this makes it even more special," he said, handing Moe the letter which had come in the mail that morning.

Moe quickly scanned the official-looking letter. Looking up from the letter, he said, "This means more to me than the plaque and all the spareribs I ate put together." Moe Junior had been accepted to the police academy.

"Did we really surprise you?" asked Louise after his family left.

"Sure did. I don't know how you kept me from getting wind of it with all the people involved. It was a very gracious thing for the people of the town to do, letting me know that they appreciate what I do."

"You deserved every bit of it, and I want to thank you for being an excellent boss and letting me work for you all these years."

Louise's sensuality had not faded as she grew older. Even after nursing four children in a span of six years, her supple body still commanded the stares of males as she walked down the street. She was married to a postman. They met one day as he was depositing letters in the mailbox on her front porch. He had fallen in love with her the instant she smiled at him. No one had ever treated her with so much honor and respect. Two months later they were married. Their seeds of love fell on fertile ground, producing four children.

Louise was content with life. She enjoyed being a mother, even though raising her four children and working part-time kept her on a hectic schedule. Her husband supported her in a style of living far beyond what she had been accustomed to, and he worshipped the ground she walked on. He suggested that she could quit working, but she enjoyed the diversion. How would the chief ever get along without her anyway? He couldn't even keep the files in order.

"I've got all the paperwork done, Chief. If you don't have anything for me to do, I think I'll get some things from the grocery store before it's time to pick up the kids at the sitter's. That way I can surprise my husband and have supper ready when he gets home."

"Sure, I can handle things here. I plan on closing up a little early anyhow. I want to get home and have a beer with my son to celebrate his acceptance to the academy."

"Give him my congratulations again. I know how proud you are of him. He's going to be a chip off the old block."

Walking north on Main Street, Louise passed the cafe where Joe had first made love to her years ago. Peering through the now boarded-up windows, she vividly remembered sitting on the edge of the counter as Joe brought his body close to her. She could still feel his urgency as he fondled her breasts. A smile played on the corners of her lips as she remembered the crashing of the sugar bowl on the floor in the ensuing excitement. It had been an exciting time of her life, leaving her with many fond memories. She wondered how Joe was now. The last she heard, he was confined to the state mental center. The urge to see him crossed her mind. A tide of desire quickly passed.

Twenty-One

Amanda was alone now. The old man had died. She had felt no remorse when her father breathed his last breath, unable to issue any more orders. She didn't even feel guilty about all the times she had wished him dead. He had been an evil man. In the end, his mind had become demented. He would rant and rave for hours on end as if demons inhabited his mind. He cursed her with defaming violence and demanded her full attention. She had always been afraid of him when he was alive, and she wondered why. She realized now that his threats had been meaningless and harmless. He was a decrepit old man who had wielded mental control over her all her life.

She was forty-nine years old now, but appeared much older. She had never been able to make herself look pretty. The old man had not permitted her to spend money on herself. She had never been to a beauty shop. Her cloths were frumpy dresses that she bought off the bargain counter. Her facial features had never been highlighted by make-up. What would she do now? There was no one to talk to. No family to be with. There had been only two people she valued in life—Joe, her ex-husband, and their son Tad. If Tad had lived he would have been thirty-four years old. I could have been a grandmother, she thought as she envisioned rocking a small child in her arms.

She kept all of Tad's paintings. They graced the walls of his room in the basement. Most of them were of animals, and somehow he had created them with smiling faces. The few human figures he sketched in charcoal were sad and forlorn. It was as if he found beauty and happiness in nature, but discontent in his fellow man. The death of Tad had been a great loss to her. She had grieved privately in her own room, afraid to openly express her sorrow, lest the old man explode into one of his tirades about everyone suffering for their sins.

She had loved Joe in her own way. Thinking he would provide an escape for her from her domineering father, she had encouraged him that night to make love to her. Things hadn't worked out that way. She had been very angry at Joe when he left, but she realized that no matter who she had married, her father would have driven them away. Tad had been the only expression of their love that existed.

Very few people were at the service. Amanda recognized most of them. They were older people, people who had been business associates of her father early on. When the service was over an elderly gentleman approached her. She recognized Mr. Winegart, her father's lawyer. He made periodic calls to the house to talk to her father. "Madam, I want to extend my deepest sympathy for the loss of your father. I don't want to rush things so soon after his death, but in the next couple of days you can come to my office for the reading of your father's will."

Three days later, Amanda listened to the monotonous drone of the old lawyer's voice as he read the formal dictation of the will. "Being of sound mind, I leave all my earthly possessions to my only living kin, Amanda."

"What possessions could he possibly have?" Amanda asked. "He complained constantly about being on the verge of financial ruin. He feared losing the house, and being forced to live off the state to survive."

"Your father's estate is quite large, Miss Amanda. It involves a sizable bank account plus numerous investments in land and business operations. I can't at this time tell you the exact worth, but it's upwards of at least two million dollars."

Stunned, she looked down at her shoes with the heels almost worn off, her homely dress, and her age-worn purse. "The bastard," she uttered. He had forced her to live in poverty all these years when he could have well afforded to let her have a few luxuries in life.

Amanda admired the reflection in the mirror. The new navy suit gave her an air of respectability. Her hair was cut and styled, and a hint of make-up accented the frail features of her face. She hoped Joe would notice. She drove to the state mental center once a week to see him. Some days he was able to come to the visiting room. Other days they would only let her peer at him through the small observatory window in the door of the isolation room. She hoped he would be well enough today for her to talk to him.

"You look pretty today," said Joe, as the orderly guided him to the chair across the table from her. "What's in the sack?"

"I brought you some things. I hope you like them and can use them."

Joe eagerly took the items from the sack: a comic book, a deck of playing cards, a notebook, a bottle of after-shave lotion, and a pair of argyle socks. "Thank you, Rosie, I'll be the envy of everyone here."

She didn't correct him. "My father passed away. Do you remember him?" she asked.

He stared into space. A feeling of anger came over him. He couldn't identify it, but it burned deeply into his past.

"You are cordially invited to attend the graduation ceremonies..." Moe read the invitation with pride. His son was graduating from the police academy, ranking top in his class. He had always hoped Moe Junior would follow in his footsteps, but had never pressured him to do so. One of the instructors at the academy was an old friend of Moe's. "That son of yours is a natural," he told Moe. "He's bright and intuitive, but more important, he's got a lot of street sense for someone so young. He must have inherited it from you."

Over the years it had become difficult for Moe to think of his son as being adopted. Looking at them, anyone would assume they were father and son because of their similar features. Moe Junior's personality and mannerisms were a mirror reflection of his father's. Moe was proud of him. He would be a good policeman. Moe's hope was that his son could find a position in some large city in the state, getting experience that would make him eligible for the position of chief of police of Laynard when he retired. He made a mental note to subtly plant the idea in the minds of the city council, especially those members that owed him a favor.

The road sign indicated the state mental care center was thirty-two miles left at the next intersection. "Would you mind making a short detour and driving past the mental care center?" asked Louise. They were returning from their summer vacation. The four children were sleeping in the back of the station wagon. Her husband rubbed his eyes trying to relieve the burning caused by the bright sunlight.

"What could there possibly be there that you would want to see?"

"I heard that someone I knew a long time ago is a patient there. Since I don't ever come up this way, I thought I should drop in and at least say hello to him."

The clerk in the administration office looked questionably

at Louise when she asked if Joe was confined to the center. "I don't ever remember you visiting him before. Are you a relative? For the last fifteen years he has only had one person that comes to visit."

"We were friends a long time ago," said Louise, with a blush coloring her cheeks.

"You know he's mentally insane."

"Not really, I had no idea. Can I talk to him a few minutes?"

"He's confined to an isolation cell."

"Can I at least see him?"

"Well, I guess we could let you look at him through the window. If he's having a good day, you may even be able to converse with him."

The hair on the back of her neck bristled as the security guard led her down the corridor. Her footsteps echoed on the stone floor. Suddenly, there was a scream sounding like a wounded animal. It was followed by a crescendo of moaning. "They're sorta restless today," said the guard.

They stopped in front of a door with a small window at eye level. A heavy metal mesh covered the opening. "Someone here to see you," said the guard as he rattled his large key ring against the mesh.

Louise peered through the mesh. The acrid stench of urine penetrated the air. The room was bare except for a wooden cot securely bolted to the wall. A crumpled figure, dressed in institutional blue shirt and pants, lay on the cot. His eyes were fixed on the opening in the door.

"Hello, Joe." The figure made no response. The only recognition was a brief contraction of the pupils of his eyes.

As Louise turned to leave, large tears of pity filled her eyes.

"Did you see your friend?" asked her husband when she returned to the car.

"No, I was mistaken. He wasn't there."

Reality blended with illusions and became one. His mind

became a pool of fantasies. Joe's mind teetered between sanity and insanity. The subconscious took preponderance over the conscious, dredging up long-suppressed guilt. The black spider roamed freely now, exuding its venom and weaving a massive web, securely entrapping its prey. Images appeared, then melted away, blending with others, evoking memories from the past. The metamorphosing of the bloody body by the side of the road suddenly became Tad and pictures of animals with smiles on their faces danced around him in an angelic manner. The pictures turned to huge, heavy drops of blood that fell on him and suffocated him. All logic had been destroyed.

Twenty-Two

Ex-Chief of Police Moe Hendersen patiently pecked out words on the keys of the old manual typewriter. Heaps of crumpled paper surrounded his desk. He was working on his third novel.

He started the first one before he retired. His work was fiction, but it was laced with incidents and experiences he had had in his years of law enforcement. He built his stories around the concept that justice always prevails, even though it may not be evident at the time. There was a force in the universe that impartially judged all men's actions, meting out punishment for their misdemeanors.

Moe had retired early. His desire to write, and the long stressful hours of his job as chief of police, slowly began to erode the enthusiasm he had for law enforcement. When this began to happen he realized that his effectiveness would suffer. Not wanting to chance losing the reputation he had enjoyed in the town of Laynard, he submitted his resignation.

The city council was stunned by his request. They considered him to be one of the top police chiefs in the state. However, after he explained his reasons, they were sympathetic to his action. They requested his recommendations for a replacement. He submitted a list of names which included his son, Moe Junior.

They questioned him about his son being a viable candidate for the position. "Doesn't Moe Junior have a good position on the force in Knox?" asked the chairman.

"Yes, but I think he would be interested in the position if you recruited him. Laynard is his home."

The council was elated when Moe Junior accepted the position of chief of police in the town of Laynard. He had graduated from the academy three years previously at the top of his class.

His personnel record from the Knox police force identified him as a model officer excelling in the field of investigation. Moe volunteered to stay on the job part-time for three months at no salary to help his son become oriented to his new position. The transition had gone smoothly.

Moe Junior respected the vast knowledge he could glean from his father's years of experiences, and they worked together as colleagues instead of father and son.

Maria punched in her time card. It read 11:28 P.M. She held the honor of being the longest-employed nurse at the state mental care center. She had just recently requested the late-night shift so she could baby-sit her two granddaughters in the afternoon. She hurried down the corridor, knowing the young nurse on duty would complain if she had to remain at her post even a few seconds past her allotted time.

As she passed isolation room #37, she peeked in to see if her friend Joe was asleep. He was laying in a fetal position on the floor. *As soon as I get checked in and am sure everything* is in order, I'll have to come back and put him in bed, she thought.

She had only been working at the center for two weeks when Joe had been admitted. A bond of friendship had formed between them from the very beginning. Early on, when he had periods of apparent mental stability, she developed a strong physical attraction toward him.

She encouraged his sexual overtures, standing close to his bed so he could reach under her uniform and run his hands up between her thighs. One night when she was making a bed check, she found him awake. It was evident that he was sexually aroused. He had pleaded with her to get into the bed with him. The fear of getting caught and losing her job was not worth the chance. Standing close to the bed, she let his hand move all the way up between her thighs.

Slipping her hand under the blanket, she had quickly relieved him. "Thanks, Rosie," he said with a sigh.

The young nurse on duty was looking at her watch as Maria approached the nurse's station. "Anything unusual going on?" ask Maria.

"Did you notice a full moon outside tonight?" the nurse replied. "Something really has them stirred up. I haven't been able to sit down once since I've been on duty. I've had to have the security people up here a couple of times. I didn't have time to write up any records, so that's still left to be done."

The third floor ward turned into a riot during the late shift that night. One patient had set his bed on fire with matches that must have been slipped to him by a visitor. Another had defecated all over himself, and Maria had to bath him and replace his bedding. It was the wee hours of the morning before she found time to write up the records from the shift before. Most of the patients had finally settled down, but there were still frequent moans and screams from the ward.

Maria was glad to see her replacement coming down the hallway. "It's been one of those nights," she said, "but I think things have finally settled down."

As she checked out of the security desk, she remembered

Joe. She had been so busy that she didn't have time to check on him during her shift. "Can I have the key to room #37?" she asked the security guard. "I want to check on a patient before I leave."

When she peered through the meshed opening of the door to room #37, she saw Joe still lying on the floor in a fetal position. She unlocked the door, and as she approached the figure on the floor, a large black spider scurried for the safety of darkness under the wooden cot in the corner of the room.

"Joe." She reached down and touched his forehead. It was as cold as the floor on which he lay. Tears of thankfulness filled her eyes. He was finally free of mental torment.

Moe Hendersen, Jr., Chief of Police, eased himself into the large swivel chair that his father had sat in so many years. He admired the carved wooden plaque on the desk. His father had given it to him. It read, "Seek Justice." He felt at home in this office. He had spent so much time here with his father as he was growing up. He remembered the rides in the police car and how his greatest thrill was when his father let him turn on the siren as they drove down Main Street.

The last two days he had been going through all the files his father kept. He must have kept a record of every ticket he ever wrote. There were stacks of files on the desk. Most of them could be thrown away, but he wanted to go through them in case there were any documents that might be of importance.

The name on the top file was almost faded beyond recognition. He peered closely and made out the name, Roy Lee. The contents of the file were yellow with age. The date indicated that it was over twenty years old. The contents included a photograph with dried stains of blood. It was a picture of a cowboy on a bucking Brahma bull. Written on the back were the words, "To my friend Roy Lee, Tex Oakes."

Scanning the entries made in the file, he sensed the frustration his father must have had trying to solve the case, unable to find any clues to indicate a suspect. All these years had gone by and the individual that had been responsible for taking this young boy's life apparently had kept it a secret.

I wonder if justice was ever served, thought Moe Junior as he closed the file.

Three figures stood beside the open pit, each with their own private thoughts about the man in the casket. Louise thought about the exciting time they had had together at the old log cabin. Amanda wondered how different things would have been if her father hadn't badgered Joe to the point of leaving her and their child. Maria thought of the slow, painful death he had endured. They all heard the words of the minister as he read from the scriptures: "Vengeance is mine, saith the Lord…"